B81/23

D1270524

WE ARE ALL SO GOOD AT SMILING

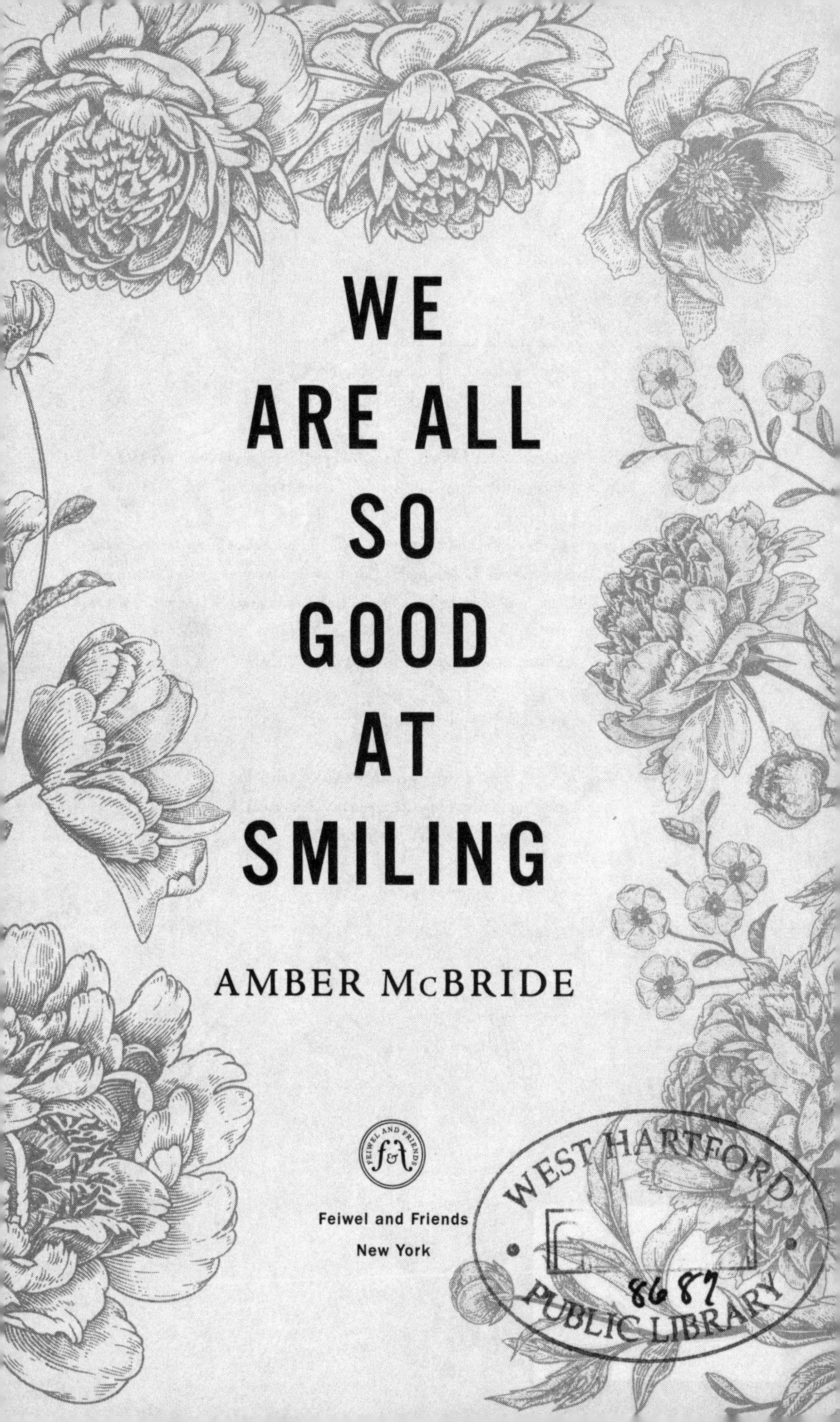

WE ARE ALL SO GOOD AT SMILING

AMBER McBRIDE

Feiwel and Friends
New York

A FEIWEL AND FRIENDS BOOK
An imprint of Macmillan Publishing Group, LLC
120 Broadway, New York, NY 10271 • fiercereads.com

Our books may be purchased in bulk for promotional, educational, or business use. Please contact your local bookseller or the Macmillan Corporate and Premium Sales Department at (800) 221-7945 ext. 5442 or by email at MacmillanSpecialMarkets@macmillan.com.

Library of Congress Control Number: 2022034723

First edition, 2023

Book design by Michelle McMillian
Feiwel and Friends logo designed by Filomena Tuosto
Printed in the United States of America

ISBN 978-1-250-78038-6

1 3 5 7 9 10 8 6 4 2

A Note Before Entering the Forest

We Are All So Good at Smiling deals with topics that might be triggering to some. This book borrows from my personal experiences with clinical/major depression. It tries to articulate that feeling of living in the *real* world, but also totally outside of it, often feeling that a part of you has been taken away & hidden. Clinical depression, self-harm & suicide are all topics that are addressed in *We Are All So Good at Smiling* & if those topics are triggering for you, this might not be the best book for you to read at this time. I know clinical depression made me play false narratives in my head & often I pretended to be fine (always smiling) when I actually felt like I was wandering through a haunted Garden of my own creation. I wrote this book to remind myself there is a way out, there are tools I can utilize, there are people who care—there are doctors who can help. I hope it can remind you, too. I empathize with feeling a pain rooted so deep that you can't separate from the ache. I want you, reader, to know I see you, your pain is valid & it is real. I don't know you, but I care. I care so much & I wish you every happiness & all the Fairy Tale endings, but mostly I hope that whenever you find yourself in Sorrow's Garden—you have tools & you can find a way out.

This book is dedicated to you—I see you.
I am always wishing you well.

So when I think of autumn, I think of somebody with hands
who does not want me to die.
—TONI MORRISON, *The Bluest Eye*

come celebrate with me that everyday
something has tried to kill me and has failed.
—LUCILLE CLIFTON, "won't you celebrate with me"

Narrator (Interlude)

A Fairy Tale rarer than Middlemist's Red blooms—
a Conjurer & a Fae, soaked in sorrow,
a Forest holding a Garden
filled with stories & magic
where memories unweave
unravel & (sometimes)
trap us in lies.
Make us
want to
die.

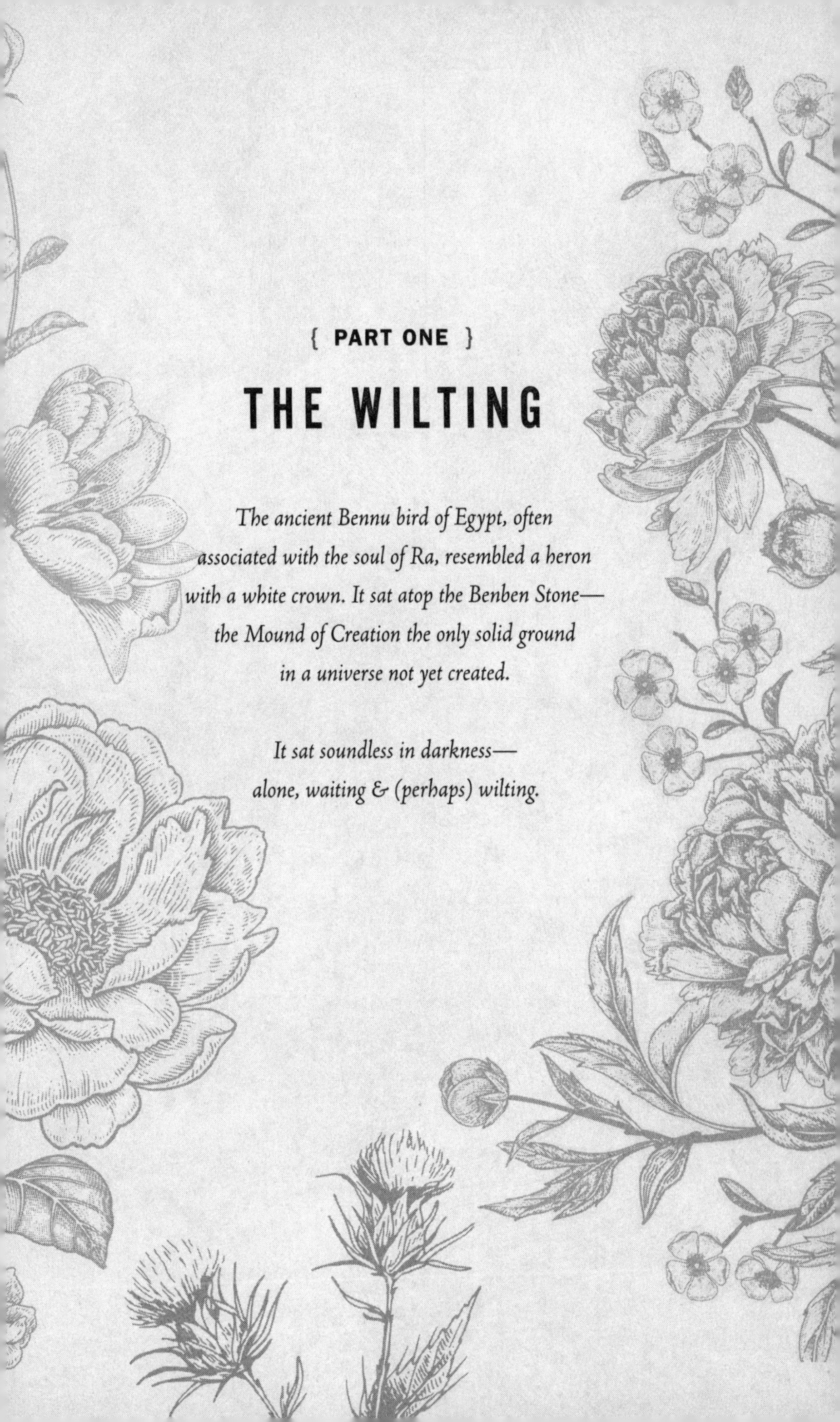

{ PART ONE }

THE WILTING

The ancient Bennu bird of Egypt, often associated with the soul of Ra, resembled a heron with a white crown. It sat atop the Benben Stone—the Mound of Creation the only solid ground in a universe not yet created.

It sat soundless in darkness—alone, waiting & (perhaps) wilting.

Call Me Magic: Call Me (Whimsy)

This is what I know:
my name is Whimsy & magic is real—
a fine glitter hovering in the air.
It doesn't matter that most can't see the energy (the ashe)
like a woven spell stringing through & connecting all things.
It doesn't matter that some don't believe in magic,
they still inhale it.
They are still part of the plucked heart-thrum of life.
You see,
the non-magical look & look & don't see.
Still, there are things that cross magic lines.
Sadness can seep into anything, even trees
especially the weeds—perhaps (even)
a soul.

This is something true:
ever since I was three feet tall
I've had the same uniform—
a pair of Converse shoes, black with little white skulls
kissing the tops,
a pair of black jeans worn at the knees from kneeling
in the weeds.
A black T-shirt never tucked in, always lazily hanging,
a tiny necklace with quartz at the center
that Grandma gave me.
I wear black sunshades that hold back
unspun licorice curls

& leather gloves on full moon days
to hide my glowing palms.
Last, always dirt & my Fairy Tale
notebook in tow.

This is something difficult:
I am here (again) in the hospital,
& my uniform changes—
no jewelry (they took my quartz necklace).
White shirt (they confiscated my black one).
White pants (my black ones had too many pockets).
White shoes (that show too much dirt).
Gloveless, bookless, dirt-less & moonless.
Feeling less, less, less.

This is the thing,
sometimes it gets bad, roots mingle with a strange soil
& you don't trust your hands with your skin.
Sometimes that means you are admitted to a hospital.
To be watched & watched & watched & watched.
To talk & talk & talk & talk—
to sometimes break.

It's like Grandma said to me when I sat, legs crossed
like cherry stems, at the edge of the Forest where toothy fog
had already begun to seep into the soil—
Hoodoo is real, witches & Fae people too.

Fairy Tales are real,
magic is real, but, careful, Whimsy,
sometimes your own mind will unroot you.

This is what I think:
I am (Whimsy): I am magic just like my name.
But I am not whimsical (anymore).

PROLOGUE

HOSPITAL

THE WHIMSY GIRL

Ashe Child:
A child loved by the supernatural
& glittering with magic. In Hoodoo,
ashe is the magic in all things.

Outside My Hospital Window

It's cloudy (inside me) & outside the window
with bars & netting that basically yell,
Don't even try escaping.

It all started with a 3-day hospital stay
then Mom & Dad (Jill & Jack) moved me
to a private facility for *extra care*
for 2 more weeks—14 days.

Day 1: busy schedule from 7 a.m.–7 p.m.
Day 2: same thing with an *evaluation* & new meds.
Days 3, 4, 5, 6 & 7: same schedule, less hazy
on the (inside) & outside.

Here's the thing,
my hands have not handled
the earth in 7 days, which is a different
kind of sadness.

It's 6 a.m. & I wake from the usual nightmare
that even sleeping pills don't dull—
the one where I try to play the goddess
& make dead things more alive. The one where
a shadow crams dirt down my throat & twigs replace
my hands & some Ursula has taken my voice,
so none of my spells stick to the air right.

I look down, my palms glow amber-golden
on account of the full moon. It's strange to still glow—
    days after perhaps, maybe, wanting to die.

Car (Silver) Like a Broadsword

In the distance an engine purrs
& my feet hit the ice-cold hospital floor
thinking Mom & Dad might be here early, for their visit.

Beyond the window with steel netting
a large gray owl & a smaller white one
sit perched on a slim tree limb—
looking wiser than even the stories claim.
    I worry the branch might break with their weight
    but then again, I worry about breaking a lot.

The parking lot is dim & I watch
the horizon gently run golden
    fingers through the darkness.

It looks difficult, the night (departing) & day (arriving)—
    I imagine them begging
to hover together in this moment (forever & Fairy-Tale-ever),
never wanting to fall out of touch.

The engine revs closer.
I spot a silver car, the same hue
as a broadsword, backing into a parking spot.

The door swings open & a boy with mint-green hair
    like just-birthed forest moss
steps out (one long leg at a time).

The deep V-neck of his shirt reveals
the bloom of a flower tattoo
(creeping thistle)
I think.

I watch the sunrise rush forward
like it wants to touch him,
like it wants to hug him
& perhaps, maybe, love him.
I watch the owls on the thin tree limb
cock their heads, left then right,
when sunlight reaches them,
they spread their wings
& take flight, looking for night.

Shadow-Wings

The boy is alone
    (which is strange)
most kids don't arrive here alone.

Usually there is a mother, a father, a sibling,
a friend, a teacher, a therapist, a nurse—
    (someone, anyone) to stand & witness
the bravery of surrendering—of crossing the line.
I should know, I've done this many times.

The sunrise still shadows the mint-haired boy
outlining his trim frame & I see them
(the outline of wings) shadowed on the pavement—
                                        Fae wings.

My palms lie flat on the window—
    I want to touch them (the wings).
        I want to know him (the Fae boy).
            I want to add him (to my notebook stuffed
                                        with Fairy Tales).

His gaze climbs, laddering up
the building & lands on me,
taking in my glowing palms,
big brown eyes, dark brown skin,
& wild black curls filled
with electricity.

He removes his shades,
lets his green hair fall (like spring leaves)
into his face. His brows knit as he studies me.
He shoves his hands deep in his pockets
& tilts his head as if to say,
It's not polite to stare.

I hold his gaze as if to say,
Who is staring at who?

He shrugs, agreeing?
The dark circles under his eyes remind me of bruises,
remind me of me 7 days ago.

He enters the hospital, wings thin & wispy & wilting
(in his shadow)
with the sun greedily clinging to him—
the sun trying to love him, the Fae boy running away.

Things I Know About Fae

1. Wings like the petals of a ghost orchid.
2. Wings invisible (even to me) until called forth.
3. Invisible except when their outline shadows the pavement.
4. Which only happens during the sunrise after a full moon.
5. Bones weightless as air. Skilled in magic & battle.
6. Can be born from any magical couple.
7. Cautious about witch-work & Hoodoo.
8. Witty & willful—excellent politicians or humanitarians.
9. Rarer than a corpse flower: fiery as a flame lily.
10. As whimsical as windswept broom moss.
11. Give them an inch & they will charm you out of house & home.

Morning (Bathroom) Ritual

I get my own bathroom
because I am not high-high risk,
but a nurse has to bring
me a toothbrush, hairbrush
& a change of clothes
because (apparently)
there are limits to trust.

My shirt is (still) white.
    My pants are (still) white.
The bed is made without screws—
(like a strange folding table)
'cause screws can unscrew.

My hair is a wilderness
of black candy shoestrings
around my face.

I feel naked without my black sunglasses.
I feel worried without my leather gloves.
I feel soulless without dirt.
I feel hopeless without my notebook stuffed with Fairy Tales.

Day 8 schedule:
(before breakfast)
Mom & Dad visit then
group therapy, art time,

coping techniques,
individual therapy.

Today Mom & Dad visit—
  so, I practice my smile
in the mirror over & over again
thinking, *Mirror, Mirror,*
who is the biggest liar of them all?

If mirrors could talk
  this one would say,
    You, Whimsy.
      All you do is lie.

Mom & Dad Visit

I practice my smile down the pictureless, sterile hall (accompanied by a nurse). It's hard to hold the smile in place, I keep reminding myself to keep the edges of my mouth from falling into a scowl. I arrive at the glass door & I see them (Mom & Dad), hands laced tighter than vines buried

deep, deep,

deep in the ground.

Mom & Dad look cold, huddled together, like winter has sleighed into the room without them knowing. I think of a spell, perhaps to make it snow, so they have a reason to be freezing,
until I realize—I made Mom & Dad worry & frown.

The reason is me.

It's my fault (I froze their bones).

I step inside & they unfreeze, stand quickly,
fold me into a hug that feels like sunflower petals.
Dad holds me at arm's length.

How are you feeling?

On a scale of 1–10?
I ask, smile still plastered.

Mom says,
Answer your father.

I shrug.
I miss the dirt.

Mom tugs a flannel bag
from her purse. *I thought you might.*
It's from the creek behind our house.

I hold the flannel in my hand.
I feel the *ashe* of it seep
into my skin.
Thank you.
Thank you.

Just one more week.
Dad rubs his eyes.

I am feeling better.
Much better,
I say, smile
unlacing slightly.

Mom crosses her arms.
That's what you said last time.

I study my feet
feeling like an apple core
is stuck in my throat.

What Mom means
is they said you are not
participating in group therapy,
Dad says, watching me.

I don't like sharing.
I tap my fingers.

You don't like it here either,
do you? Mom asks.

Guilty, I say, making an X
of myself as I cross my arms.

You can't avoid this forever
or you will end up back here
again & again &...
Mom's voice trails off.

I swallow,
filling in the blanks.
Until I don't... until I am gone.

I'll try harder,
I promise.

They hear me,
because they are both sitting again
hands vined together.

Each tear a sugar cube
contaminated with salt.

All smiles melted
because of me.

Reasons It's Easier for Mom & Dad

1. Sometimes Mom uses Hoodoo to weave a spell that eats & morphs memories.
2. She can even change her own. Remember exactly what she wants.
3. She works for the government, can make anyone forget.
4. She works for the government, can make anyone unsee.
5. She has used it once on Dad (to move around details); it worked.
6. She used it once on herself (to change specifics); it stuck.
7. Mom has used it many times on me—it only took some memories.
8. I remember the hard parts because I was there . . .
9. Like the taste of the wind that day.
10. How the pine needles muffled my scream.
11. I think I remember wings. Snapped bones.
12. Knowing something happened, without the details—is easier for Mom & Dad.
13. So, when I was 14, I decided to pretend I didn't remember a thing.
14. & Mom stopped magicking me—& more details (slowly) seeped in.
15. Knowing something happened, with too many details, means everything is heavy.
16. Knowing with too many details means you don't know which memories to trust.

Break-Fast

Is a group activity.
    I un-group.

Thinking how I am (here)
(disappointing everyone)
inside my brown skin suit
topped with a crown of black
licorice hair that does not
even feel like my body anymore.

I am here even when I think,
        Perhaps, maybe,
            I should not be.

I am still here, stretched thin
through 72 seasons, 18 years—
18 falls as crisp as crumbled graham crackers.

Here,
    somehow. Still.

Sitting on this cool,
hard hospital windowsill.

I know I am Whimsy,
but when I look at my reflection
(ghostly in the window) I swear

I don't know the eyes tracking me—
    like something else entirely hides inside.

But, I am here—strapped
    in the hospital
with white cinder blocks
stacked like square Tic Tacs,
    as a precaution.

You see, this time I made a list called
Ways I could stop air from entering my lungs.

It was a very comprehensive list.

I get why Mom & Dad
brought me here for the
11th time in 10 years.

So, I am here,
hands balled into fists,
hiding from the crispest
autumn in a decade.

Air heavy in my lungs.
    Alive.
        Alive.
            Alive.

Somehow, still here.
With all these people
& strangely, alone.

The Fae (Faerry)

A shadow silhouettes in front of me—
May I sit?

No.
Mint-green hair, winged boy doesn't leave.

May I stand here?
His hands shift to his pockets.

No.
Mint-green hair, winged boy takes a step back.

How about here?
He crosses his arms in front of him.

I glare
a spell on the tip
of my lips.

You glare a lot.

You talk too much.

I start a spell
to tie his (charming) lips shut.

I wouldn't magic here.
Might earn you more pills.
He says waving an index finger
marked with a corpse flower tattoo.

Might be worth it
to wipe that smirk
off your face.

He fully smiles.
I think smirking
is just in a Fae's DNA.

Seems too joyful for here,
I say, pointing
at the steel netting
on the window.

I love to put up a façade.
I am brimming with joy.

You're not fooling anyone.
I sigh, curious.
What's your name?

Faerry.
What's your name?

You're a walking cliché.
I keep glaring at the Fae
named Faerry.
Whimsy.

We love a cliché.
He grins at me,
the Conjurer
named Whimsy.

I'll be seeing you,
Whimsy.

Faerry takes five steps backward
before he turns to find a table
to sit at alone.
His smile falls as he sits.

I shake my head thinking,
We are all so good at smiling—
like we invented it.

Group Therapy

We sit in a circle (like teenagers around a summer campfire)
    except with 11 fold-out chairs, one for each patient
& the doctor.
All we need is a real fire in the center & long sticks
with marshmallows melting & burning on them.

I don't bother with real names,
    most of these people I'll never see again.

So, I assign each person a Fairy Tale name instead.
    One; the therapist with the notepad—Baba Yaga
without the metal nose.
Two; the boy with brilliant blue hair—perhaps Bluebeard
without the dead wives.
Three; the one with long spidery legs—Anansi
without the trickery.
Four; the one who has an umbrella to block the sun—
Godmother Death, perhaps for real?
Five; the one who arrived in green sequin pants—Mama Wata
without the fins.
Six; the girl with rosy apple cheeks—Snow White
without the dwarves behind her.
Seven; the one with bright red lips—Adze
minus the drinking blood.
Eight; the one with a sore throat—Ursula without a voice.
Nine; the oldest, who has been here three times—Griot
without stories.

Ten; a boy with mint-green hair (an actual Fae, I believe)
actually named Faerry.

Eleven; the silent one with stories on her skin
& magic like electricity in her hair—
that would be Me (Whimsy).

Group Therapy: Tell Us a Secret

One; the therapist with the notepad—Baba Yaga.
(I have been sad too . . .)

Two; the boy with brilliant blue hair—Bluebeard.
(I have three girlfriends right now . . .)

Three; the one with long spidery legs—Anansi.
(I have arachnophobia . . .)

Four; the one who has an umbrella to block the sun—
Godmother Death.
(I am afraid of the dark . . .)

Five; the one who arrived in green sequin pants—Mama Wata.
(I don't know how to swim . . .)

Six; the girl with rosy apple cheeks—Snow White.
(I have never eaten an apple . . .)

Seven; one with bright red lips—Adze.
(Blood makes me faint . . .)

Eight; the voiceless one—Ursula.
(I love to sing . . .)

Nine; the oldest, who has been here three times—Griot.
(I hate stories . . .)

Ten; a Fae boy with mint-green hair, actually named Faerry.

(I hate trees . . .)

Eleven; the silent one with stories on her skin—Me (Whimsy).

(I am jealous of leaves . . .)

The therapist pauses.

Wait, why are you jealous

of leaves, Whimsy?

My Answer: Cemetery of Leaves

I answer, *I am jealous*
of things that know
what they are.

Snow White:
I don't get it.

I explain,
A leaf is always a leaf
even after it yellows,
then goldens & finally browns.

A leaf is still a leaf even when
my sneaker crushes it
into Halloween cupcake sprinkles.

Mama Wata frowns.
But then it's a crushed leaf.

Yeah, but Halloween-sprinkle-leaf
doesn't even think it is broken,
because surprise, leaves don't think.

Godmother Death chimes in:
Exactly. They don't think,
so how do they know?

I try to explain,
Leaves don't think,
but they know things.
They have intuition.

Ursula with the small voice:
Are you high? Like . . .

I roll my eyes.
Listen, a leaf is especially
still a leaf once it is swept carelessly
into the grass that is still holding on to summer
with yellow-tipped lemon drop nails.

Bluebeard with three girlfriends:
But it's dead.

I stomp my foot.
& when a leaf decays into
the soil so much it no longer looks
like a leaf, even then,
EVEN THEN
it is a leaf.

Everyone is silent & I hope they get the point
(which of course is)—a brain is still a brain
with or without serotonin—but we think too much.

We need to remember that the mind is still a mind,
floating like a newborn cloud
or bird wings drowning in hardened chocolate.

My point is that a leaf knows it's important,
at all moments of its life
even when it is broken.
People always forget
that a rough day, a bad year—
doesn't equal a bad life.

Everyone (in Therapy) Is Silent After My Soliloquy

Silence for one gumdrop . . .
two gumdrops . . .
eleven gumdrops . . .

Faerry's eyes sparkle.
So, a leaf is NOT a leaf?

I resist flicking
Faerry off.
Please fly to hell.

Faerry clears his throat
making the tiny apple
tattoo on his neck ripple.
So, what you are saying is
a baptism is still a baptism
whether it is done in milk or water?

I nod slowly.
Death is still death
by fire or ice.

A Conjurer is still a Conjurer
hands in the soil or hands laced in lap?
Faerry bites his lip.

I think we are getting off track,
the therapist interrupts.

Just like wings are still wings
hidden like a ghost orchid
or parading out in the open.
I lean back in my flimsy chair.

I understand
what you are saying, Whimsy.

No, I don't think
you do, Faerry,
I say, getting up
mostly scared
that he does
(in fact) get it.

Last Week in the Hospital

I don't like how Faerry sees through
my skin to my bones,
so, I keep sitting alone.

I don't participate in group therapy.
I meditate.
I use the techniques offered:

1. Play music.
2. Identify problem (brainstorm solutions).
3. Write positive statements (affirmations).
4. Tapping.
5. Rapping.

I take my pills,
        every day.

Faerry sneaks me 6 notes
under my door
on tiny pieces of napkin paper:

1. *Can Conjurers spin sadness into gold, Whimsy?*
2. *If they can, between us, we could be rich.*
3. *Why did you skip dinner, Whimsy?*
4. *What would we buy with all that gold?*
5. *The rain is still rain even when it is snow.*
6. *If I could give you the sun, I would, Whimsy.*

I find his door, send 1 note back:

I don't want the sun, Faerry—

I prefer the moon.

CHAPTER 1

WHIMSY COMES HOME

Tea Leaves: Hourglass
Imminent danger. RUN!

Back Home on Marsh Creek Lane

I've been home long enough for the moon to be showing off (again), blue-hueing above the sleepy streets of Marsh Creek Lane & my thoughts have gone wolf (again) roaming—needlessly crafting innocent shadows into toil & trouble.

My crystals moon-bathe on my windowsill, Pink Opal, Blue Goldstone, Tiger's Eye & Amethyst cleanse themselves, washing my negative energy from their pores. On the altar below my window, a box of herbs & a white plate with an offering.

As for Me (Whimsy), I nestle in my bed, covers pulled under my chin, inside my gray-brick house that is sandwiched, like an ice cream center, between other homes. Outside, streetlights, spaced ten feet apart, spotlight the sidewalk like a guilty crime scene.

Inside my room, notebooks gorged with stories & books stuffed with Fairy Tales sit in stacks, like scattered stumps without branches. It is strange, despite my being gone for 2 weeks, nothing has changed in my room.

Down the hall, filled with family portraits: Grandma (gone 9 years); Mom, Dad, Brother (named Cole, allegedly MIA 10 years) & Me (Whimsy). My parents sleep well with me within earshot (again). I think it is too loud; the crickets outside gossip too much.

I raise my sleep-soggy body from bed, haul open my moonlit window to yell, *Enough with the chirping. We get it, you're joyful with sound.* Of course, the crickets answer in a crescendo threatening some sort of plague.

I don't mind plagues, so I push the window all the way open & step (barefoot) onto the flat roof. I sit with my back pressed to the bricks & close my eyes & listen & listen—to the chirps & the resonant hoots of owls.

The moonbeams bathe my face, & on nights like this, when the moon is big, I swear I feel Grandma in the shimmer hugging me tightly—holding me together. It feels like Grandma was reincarnated as the yellow light of moon rays.

In a few hours, the house will yawn & wake, the crickets will hush to sleep—Mom will come into my room & say, *Honey, did you sleep well?* & watch me closely for signs. I'll say, *Yes,* with bloodshot eyes & she will know I'm lying.

I'll blame my sleeplessness on the strange moon, on the crystals vibrating loudly on my windowsill. I'll mention the ancestors visiting & wanting to talk. Mom will cross her arms & say, *The ancestors want you to rest.* I'll nod & stir my tea.

I'll think of Grandma—dirt always thick under her nails—
saying, *You have strong magic, child, it will make you feel many things.*
Grandma knew magic better than magic knew itself. She predicted
her death to the hour saying, *Here she comes, on her black horse.*

Mornings, Dad will make pancakes & fried eggs. He'll smile
widely, but it won't reach his eyes. I'll read my leaves closely before
I jump on a bus that will ferry me to hell. I'll eat & smile & push
the guilt down with syrup & juice, which makes it palatable.

I'll cleanse my crystals each full moon, dry my herbs & drink
healing teas. I'll ground barefoot & wild in the dirt, & I'll still
hurt at the root of me. I'll think of the Forest at the end of Marsh
Creek Lane & shudder.

I'll think of Grandma wasting her final words
on me saying, *Magic child, your death*
is a long way away.

My Old Notebook Stuffed with Fairy Tales

I have an old notebook gorged with my favorite Fairy Tales.
Some that Grandma taught me, some that Cole told me—
    some that I made up myself.

My old notebook is stuffed with yellow brick roads,
Anansi the spider,
        Griots, Baba Yaga (the wisest witch) & bad things living in
candy houses.
There are gray & white owls, rare flowers, Adze, voice-stealers
& voice-givers.
Sometimes the horsemen of the apocalypse trample through
the pages.

There is also a forest called Haunting Forest, with a Garden
at the center.
        The Garden holds all my sorrow & sadness.

My notebook is brimming with stories—
        Today I add a Fae boy, with mint-green hair
& shadowy wings, named (Faerry) to the wrinkled pages.

The (Haunting) Forest

We live on a one-way street
that leads to a cul-de-sac
with no suburban homes.

That's because at the end
of Marsh Creek Lane
there is a graveyard
with headstones that poke
out of the ground like tiny teeth—
        so no homes could be built there.

Beyond the graveyard is a Forest,
the largest in the county. Deep inside
the Forest is a Garden with rare flowers.
The Forest is haunted like most Forests are,
but when I was young
I didn't mind.

Me (Whimsy) & my brother (Cole)
traveled deep into the Forest (sometimes alone,
sometimes with Grandma) looking for plants,
hanging bottles filled with water to protect
the rare flowers found in the Garden
deep inside our Forest.

That was then—
now, I have not been in the Forest in 10 years.

There was a day (I almost remember
a hazy memory) when the Forest changed,
shadows swooped low pulling my hair,
vines broke free grabbing for my feet
& I yelled & yelled for help—
    but the trees moved like chess pieces (hiding the way home)
& the pine needles muffled my voice & I renamed
the Forest (Haunting Forest) because something bad
had sunk into the soil causing toil & trouble.

By the time I made it home,
    by the time Mom & Dad got to the spot
        where it all happened—
            it was too late (I am always too late).

Outside My House on Marsh Creek Lane: October 28

Dad sweeps decaying leaves into the grass.
He reminds me of a baker
topping a green cake
with ornate orange flourishes.
    My dad, the Baker of Landscapes.

The neighbor's dog yaps a few yards down
& I sit as silent as a seahorse
(in my black shades & leather gloves)
thinking about how deep a leaf can rot into the ground.

I reason—*Maybe hell's wrath is fueled by decaying leaves.*
Maybe it is all leaves from Earth's core all the way up.

Then two large feet
in white boots with tiny black skulls
magic in front of me.

Two large feet that crush golden leaves.

I know these shoes,
    I saw them on a boy
with shadow wings (Faerry)
through my hospital window.

Two cool gray eyes with golden specks.
Hair minty green, reminding me of seaweed

swaying under waves. The green waves are held back
by a pair of black sunglasses.

Faerry raises a finger
to his lips saying,
Shhhh.

I stare at him,
the Fae I met a few weeks ago,
in front of me telling me to *shhh.*

The moon was a full owl eye in the sky
last night & I notice Faerry avoids the sun,
so his shadow won't give him away.
Just like I wear black gloves to hide
my glowing palms.

Dad walks over
gives Faerry
the Black man dap hug.
I saw your parents
(Tristan & Isolde)
moving in a few weeks ago.

They said they had a son—
but you were on a vacation with friends.

Faerry steps back:
Nice to meet you, sir.
Yes, I was away.

I cough:
Away where?

Faerry tilts his head back,
actually laughs.
White Tower somewhere
not that fun, 10 out of 10
would not recommend.

I bite my tongue
offering myself pain
to keep from smiling:
Were there guards
in this tower?

Several. Faerry whispers,
& there was this witchlike girl.

Fascinating.
I grind my teeth.
Did you know
calling a Conjurer
a witch is rude?

Are we being polite?
Faerry folds his arms
like a layered cake.

Dad interrupts:
Don't mind Whimsy,
she likes stories,
but I think you will be
at the same high school.

Not many Black kids,
maybe she can show you around.

I am not listening, I am thinking of leaves (again)—
I wonder how many leaves it takes,
stacked one on top of the other,
to get from the center of the earth
all the way up to the crumbled Oreo topsoil.

I think, *Here's an idea,*
maybe I can climb out of hell
with stairs crafted from leaves.

Faerry (Still Annoying): On Marsh Creek Lane

Miss me?

I don't answer.

Whatever you are thinking about
seems mighty important.

Faerry sits next to me.

Your dad seems nice.

Faerry slips from the stoop,
kneeling, collecting a brilliant golden leaf.

I don't answer.
I am calculating.
I know that
100 leaves
make an inch.

100 dead crisp things
make an inch.

1,200 leaves
make one foot.

Ignoring Faerry (still),
I pull out my phone to Google
the distance to the center
of the earth (about 4,000 miles).

Depends on the leaf,
but give or take several billion leaves.
Not very sturdy stairs.

Faerry un-stoops. Hands in pockets.

Lucky guess? You were staring at leaves
& gave your leaf speech a few weeks ago.

My mouth hangs open,
my tongue is unable
to blow out words.

If you keep gaping, you might catch a fly.
You know the story about the woman
who swallowed a fly, don't you?

Faerry rolls up his sleeves & floral tattoos
(honeysuckle, snapdragon & angelica root)
bloom up his muscular arms.

He says,
You have a leaf
in your licorice hair,
may I get it?

I nod, slowly.
He accidentally steps
in the sun & his shadow
shows his secret—wings.

Faerry untangles the leaf from my curls
then purposefully crushes it under his shoe
before crouching to inspect it, reading the crumbs like a prophecy.

I unglue my mouth.
That's not how you read leaves, Faerry.

Faerry's finger pokes the crushed
leaf before he looks up, tears catching,
trapped in his lashes.
You like leaves, but you're afraid of Forests too?

I stare.
He stares back
pulling down his sleeves
covering the garden
on his arms
screwing his jaw shut.
He pulls his black shades
back over his strange eyes.

Then he walks past my dad,
across the street & into his house—
wings wilting behind him.
(If I could see them),
I am sure they would be dragging on the ground,
collecting decaying golden leaves.

What (I Think) Faerry Does Next

Because my name is Whimsy,
& I like stories, in my mind
I monologue what I *think*
Faerry does next:

With legs that long,
you go up the stairs
two at a time
to your room
which is (of course)
painted black.

You throw off your sweater
& with short sleeves on,
the garden tattooed on your arms
can be seen & the light from
the window shows your shadow
with wings, wings,
wilting wings.

I also can only assume,
by the way you sipped my thoughts
like tasty cocoa,
you are either intuitive
or you light candles

& offer blood to some devil—
do Fae worship devils, Faerry?

I bet you are the kind of boy who
burns leaves before they are even dead.
Which is not cool:
Rule One of Hoodoo,
let living things thrive.

Are you thriving, Faerry?
I think you are pretending
(like I am pretending)
to be good at smiling.

Tell me, why do you have a garden tattooed,
vining up your sleeves, if you are afraid
of a gathering of trees?

You're wrong, Faerry. I don't mind Forests,
it's just the one Forest, the Haunting one
with a Garden in the center
at the end of Marsh Creek Lane,
that I wander the edge of, but never enter—
for reasons, Faerry.

Don't worry, if you are afraid.
I won't let the Forest

eat your annoying soul,
as long as you stop sipping
my thoughts, Faerry.
You won't like what you find.

Rule Two of Hoodoo,
don't take without an offering.
What are you offering me, Faerry?

Marsh Creek Lane (Home)

Eventually,
Dad gets tired from raking
which doesn't take long nowadays
when he is stressed from worrying about me.

We go inside.
Mom is at her desk
    back as straight as a board
going through hospital & prescription costs.

I go up to my room,
taking the stairs one step at a time,
because my legs are short & don't stretch like taffy.
I take off my black leather gloves & my palms glow dully.

My room, at the moment, doesn't have a door,
    because the doctor says,
Just to be safe & no sharp objects.
So, my door is now just a movable sea
        of green beads offering privacy
but no silence.

I tug my English homework from my backpack
because I am supposed to write a 2-page essay
on Fairy Tales for my first day back
(my teacher emailed the homework
so I would not fall behind).

I am not a fan of essays & paragraphs.
Instead, I'll write a poem.
My English teacher will accept it,
I know this because I overheard her
with other teachers
before I went to the
hospital, saying,
I hear that she's severely depressed.
    I think someone died?
I'll just pass her, I don't need
tragedy on my hands.

I want to say, *The doc says I am fixed now.*
I only said I wanted to die,
I didn't actually try.
I just made a list of ways,
hid it like a pea under my mattress
& Mother found it.

It's not like my sadness
can infect other students
but they wrote a note to my mother
saying they'd seat me in the back,
have me work alone
    because people think what they want.

Just like I think, *It's just a list,*
I only thought about
the ways I could make
the air leave me forever.

& my doc thinks, *A list is very serious.*
It's very serious, Whimsy. We are admitting you.

& my therapist thinks,
You might have created
a false memory—
you're the only one who remembers
the events of that day that way.

She claims,
You are avoiding.

Luckily because of nondisclosure laws
my therapist can't tell Mom & Dad
what I actually remember.

Still, she is wrong.
I am the only one trying
to remember it right.

CHAPTER 2

FAIRY TALES: FAERRY TALES

Tea Leaves: Kettle
A sure sign of death
no matter how much you tip the cup.

What's Wrong with a Monster?

Whimsy's Fairy Tale Essay/Poem

It's all Fairy Tales; The Girl in the Tower,
The Secret Garden, the princess sleeping
on top of a tower of mattresses who feels a pea
& then gets saved by a boy on a gray horse
wielding the magic a wizard taught him.

It's all a Fairy Tale; Frankenstein building a monster
the monster, perhaps, building children.
The children roaming the earth, crouched low,
their tongues wetting the earth.
In one tale, their bellies might
ripen the dirt for farmers. In another,
they might start a plague.

There is a Griot out there granting sight
by stealing eyes & replacing them
with spit-shined marbles strapped
in with red shoestrings
because Fairy Tales require sacrifice.

Stolen Africans on guilty ships jumped overboard
because freedom was better than chains & thus
they grew wings & flew back to the Motherland
because Fairy Tales are hopeful.

There is a Banshee somewhere
telling the time of death by
clicking her tongue
& there is a man somewhere
ripping off his ears
(offering them to crows)
to un-hear the tune
because Fairy Tales offer punishment.

I am sure there is a symphony
of dead sailors at the edge
of the world, at the bottom of the sea
who can play a death hymn
for the earless man who is forced
to know fear, forced to hear
his own last breath
because Fairy Tales have villains.

A goddess in an arctic ocean
has blue hair that often storms gray.
She is as peaceful as whalebone,
but responsible for every shipwreck
because Fairy Tales are balanced.

It's all a Fairy Tale; there is a Forest
with a Garden at the end of Marsh Creek Lane.

It holds all of my pain, sorrow & sadness—
    but still sometimes it haunts me
because I am the monster, the bad person, the villain
in this Fairy Tale, because I left.

Tilt the light, follow the yellow brick road,
all the stories are a riddle for something else.

Even this.
    Especially this.

I Like My Poem

I like my poem because I love stories
just like my brother, Cole, did.

When I was young & sad, Cole said,
Tell yourself a story,
bring yourself back to you.
& he gave me a notebook to write in.

Then we'd race barefoot through the Forest,
pick flowers in the Garden until the moon rose
& Cole (10 years older) would say, *Whimsy, sometimes it feels like*
I am here but not at all—like in another dimension,
like hell, but cold & damp & foggy.

& my 8-year-old self would say,
Don't think about that,
think about: How many leaves stacked
one on top of the other does it take
to reach the moon?

Sometimes I wish I hadn't said that,
now I wish I'd said,
Tell me more, help me understand.

Doorbell Rings: Faerry on My Stoop Again

Your dad said we have the same English class.
What's the homework? I thought I might get ahead.
His gray eyes hover, looking at my sleepless ones.

We're writing an essay on Fairy Tales,
if they are important or not.
If they are childish or not.
If they are true or not.

By the way,
when did you move here?

Ironic. All things considered.
Is that yours? Faerry points to my notebook
rolled into a cylinder. *Can I read?*
His slim hand waits midair—gently asking.

I am asking when you arrived, Faerry.

A month ago.
I saw you a few times
at the edge of the Forest
collecting dirt.

I hand him my notebook
stuffed with Fairy Tales.
You didn't say hi?

I'll always say hi
from now on.
Pinky promise.

My hands find my hips.
That doesn't change
the missed hi's.
What if you never
got the chance?

Faerry pauses.
Hi, hello, hola, bonjour . . .

I guess you were busy
with your thoughts too.
Looking down, suddenly I find
my fingernails fascinating.

October is a difficult month for me.

Same.

The season is still golden . . .

Whether we splatter sadness
on the leaves or not,
I say, kicking the ground.

Don't say sadness too much, Whimsy
everyone will think we are cliché.
Faerry rolls his eyes knowingly.

The world is messed up.
Imagine, a word like sadness
being called cliché,
I say, glancing at Faerry.

If you use a word too much
they say it becomes cliché.
He raises a finger.
Love, hope, rage—sadness.

I nod.
I am very sad.

Me too,
Faerry says.

Faerry Reads My Poem

Faerry's eyes glitter reading my poem
& I wonder if his wings are like his eyes.

He moves his shirt, scratching his shoulder,
& more of his garden flashes into view
(black water iris mixed with John the Conqueror root).

You wrote a Fairy Tale.
        Faerry sits & starts to write.
His green hair reflecting the light.

The sky blinks tonight & the outside lamps
flicker on like fireflies finding homes in mason jars.
Two owls (gray & white) sit on the fence
soaking up the moon.

It's cold but heat radiates from Faerry's golden skin.
There is no frost where he sits concentrating on his homework.

His shoulder accidentally grazes mine as he writes furiously.
His shoulder offering more warmth than I have felt in years.

Want to read? Faerry bumps
    my arm with his. *Your poem inspired me.*
I think he knows his touch is like a blanket
or maybe that is just his wing cradling my shoulders.

I READ . . .

Faerry's Fairy Tale Essay/Poem

Fall is an angry season with yellowing teeth as bright as sunrise. In this Fairy Tale, there are some, built different, conceived by a magic trick. They seed the world with enchantment but even they sometimes fall like pennies in a well & their minds drown.

There is a boy who has lost & found himself so many times, he marks each rebirth with a flower making a garden on his body but he also forgets to water himself. Legends say the boy has a soul that was marked unholy, his lungs light as air from a Fae father, ribs of a witch from his mother.

Each breath he takes is a coffin approaching, a cicada hissing—his parents think he is pretending. They say, *You are too strong for this sadness, you have to move on.* But they remember things wrong. He was there, he knows the truth.

You know, Frankenstein thought himself a god saying, *I'll make a human.* God blistered & bothered in the stars saying, *How about a mind plague for humankind? We could call it Clinical Depression.*

Then they handed it out, like spoiled candy.

Good Night, Faerry

Our essays join at the hip,
I say, squinting to see Faerry
in the dark.

We both have a firm understanding of Fairy Tales.
Faerry looks down at the front of the notebook.
Fairy Tale Notebook?

I grab my notebook
that Faery has added to.
I just like stories.

Faerry glances at the Forest
at the end of Marsh Creek Lane.
Why don't you go in the Forest
for dirt for your Hoodoo work?

I stand to stretch my legs.
It's haunted.

By what?
Faerry stretches
his shirt lifts showing more vines.
Goblin? Demon? Bad witch?

By a ghost.
I glance at the unmoving Forest.

Just the one?
Faerry rubs his hands together,
they glow like a dull moon.

Is there ever just one?

Will you show me the edge of the Forest one day?
Faerry looks up at me a beat too long.
I mean only if you want . . . it feels familiar.

I thought you were afraid of forests.
I frown.

Gotta face your fears, I guess.
Will you keep me safe?

Sure, I mean if it's just the edge
of the Forest.

Thank you. Faerry dusts his hands off
& shimmers fall. He digs deep in his
pocket, pulls out a locket & hands it to me.

What's this?

The moon. He turns to leave
but (at the same time) also waves saying,
Hi, hello, bonjour . . .

I thought you were leaving?
I start for the door
locket in my hand.

I am, I am, but I've just decided . . .
he says (eyes glittering).
We never say goodbye.

I glare at his knowing smirk.
Bye, Faerry.

Please say hi. I hate goodbyes. I've had too many.
Faerry kneels on the sidewalk.

You are shameless, aren't you?
My hand flirts with the door handle.
Hello, Faerry.

Faerry un-kneels.
I like your soul,
why are you so soulful, Whimsy?

Bonjour, Faerry.
I twist the doorknob
to go inside my
wedding cake house.

Locket

I take the stairs one at a time
        swipe the beads away
& sit at the altar in front of my window.

The moon is one day less full.
I look down at the tips
of my fingers—
        they glow dully.

I gently pry open the silver locket
Faerry handed me.

Inside is a tiny moonstone.

He got me the moon—
        in a silver (locket) platter.

& for a moment I feel like there is something
I should remember—
but then Dad calls me for dinner
& I pull the locket over my head
& run down the stairs (one at a time).

Dinnertime Chat

What did the boy want?
Mom asks, unnaturally hostile.

He wanted to know
the homework for class,
I say between chews.

You know Fae don't like us,
Dad says. Sounding off.

You are the one
who was nice to him, Dad.
My fork scratches the plate.
Besides, Black kids
gotta stick together. Remember?

Dad shrugs. *I dunno,*
something feels off
about that family.

Be careful with Fae,
Mom says.
Be careful with witches.

He seems nice.
I fiddle with my locket
surprised, my parents
have never judged
like this before.

Where did you get that?
Dad asks, frowning.

Found it,

I lie.

Mom shakes her head.

It reminds me

of something.

Dad frowns.

Me too.

Weird,

I say.

Mom's magic only took some of my memories

& I get the feeling this might be one of them.

I get the feeling that we all feel like

we should remember something—

like a shadow wants to break free

in our memories.

Sleep, Nightmare, Wake, Repeat

Dinner is over,
Faerry is gone,
& I remember
I am not a good sleeper.

I worry, so I make tea & read
the leaves—an hourglass (again).

The energy feels off,
so I grab a lemon
from the kitchen
& cut it in four slices
to place in each corner
of my room before
I climb into bed.

Often when I sleep
I cross my arms over my chest.
I think of a sliver of my soul
being deep in the ground.
I think, *That's not so bad*
in the ground I can hide
from memories
from pain.

I don't mind being
in the ground with the leaves

'cause no matter what,
when I fall asleep
I dream the same dream—Ursula muting my voice,
        the Forest. The Garden deep inside.

The sadness
        opens like a fault line
in the earth & I fall in every time.
        I yell, *Help me!*

But, nothing helps me,
        when I fall asleep,
                I dream the same dream
& it's always my fault.

CHAPTER 3

STONE RIDGE HIGH SCHOOL

Tea Leaves: Kite
Usually signals a long trip
that will end well.
Imagine Me (Whimsy) a kite
with a hole
hurtling to the ground.

Morning (October 29)

The sun splits my eyes apart
& the dream spills
onto my pillow.

Most mornings start like this:
cry, short shower, medication,
sometimes meditation
& more medication.

I check & the lemon slices
already have mold—
which means very bad energy.
I collect the slices in a bag to bury
at the edge of the Forest.

Then ten minutes
of mirror guilt watching myself
sob out the last of the dream.

Me crying
        me crying,
splashing cold water on my face,
saying the same thing I have chanted
to myself for several days now,
Whimsy, only a sliver
of your soul is lost
in the Forest.
    Don't let it get you.

I put my locket back on
(because I like the moon)
& take the steps
downstairs
one at a time.
Grab a Pop-Tart,
pop the pills sitting
on the unicorn napkin
& go to school
for the first time this month
still feeling heavy,
just as heavy.

Morning (October 29) Outside My House

I walk toward the bus stop slowly,
careful not to step on the cracks
in the sidewalk & perhaps cause a catastrophe.

A door swings open hitting brick & I see Faerry
eyes red & puffy. The door hits again
& I see a father (Tristan)—*Don't you ever go*
without our permission again.

Sure, I'll just hurt myself (again) instead.
Faerry opens his car door.
Worried it might hurt your approval ratings
having a son who needs help? Who is depressed?

A mom (Isolde) appears,
You act like you are the only one hurting,
but <u>*missing*</u> *does not mean* <u>*gone*</u>*—Faerry, there is hope.*

Faerry throws his backpack in his car.
You both seem to be doing just fine.

Faerry's mom goes back in the house.
Faerry's dad says, *You have pills,*
you have therapy, get it together. Black boys
don't get to be sad & feel their feelings.

I flinch at the words.
    Like it is that simple.
My palms glow angrily.

Faerry's face turns to stone,
he pulls his sunglasses over
his puffy eyes saying,
Yeah, Dad. I'll snap my fingers
    & work on that.

Faerry slides into
his silver car
like a broadsword,
pulls out the driveway
& toward high school hell.

High School

I missed some of last year too,
but with homework finished,
a perfect SAT & "special" doctor's note,
    attendance is a leaf in the wind.

The school did not always "get it" until my therapist
strutted into the school (a knight on a mission)
with a PowerPoint & a gold power suit.

It's hard to explain when you are bruise-less.

It's hard to explain,
I am so tired I have to convince myself
to breathe each breath.

I get it, I guess.
    I have everything, right?
It's the same when you follow the recipe,
but the cupcakes don't rise.
You can't put your finger on the *why*.

My therapist says, *You shouldn't have to get it,*
    empathy is fine but it is not an excuse
to understand why others treat you badly.

I tuck the copy of this week's reading,
    Inferno, under my arm.

I walk alone in the school halls
because when you leave high school
for *unknown reasons,* your friends jump ship.

In AP English, I sit in the back right corner,
beside the book poster of wooded Narnia
& try to make myself as small as a Tic Tac.

Before AP English Class

(Teacher Chat)

I read your essay/poem,
if you ever need to talk.

I don't.

If you . . .

I don't.

You are not a monster . . .

I know.

But the poem . . .

Is a metaphor.

Care to elaborate?

That's a hard nope.

I understand.

Trust me, you don't.

I hate when people say that.

Things I Hear My Classmates Say

1. *Why doesn't she just smile?*
2. *How do you get excused for being extra tired?*
3. *I must be hella depressed because I am hella tired.*
4. *I heard she ran away.*
5. *I heard she hurt someone.*
6. *How selfish.*
7. *Whimsy only loves herself.*
8. *I heard she sleeps in the dirt.*
9. *She hardly showers.*
10. *I heard she wants to die.*
11. *I heard she was hospitalized 20 times.*

Things I Hear Valda (the Bully) Say

1. *I can't believe I was ever her friend.*
2. *She is selfish.*
3. *Cost her parents so much money.*
4. *She was always strange.*
5. *She reads tea leaves & has crystals.*
6. *She is obsessed with Fairy Tales.*
7. *I wish she would just disappear.*
8. *I heard she got in trouble with the law.*
9. *Her parents covered it up.*
10. *Are you going to cry, Whimsy?*
11. *Why don't you go cry, Whimsy?*

Inferno by Dante

Is not a Fairy Tale technically,
but it is a tale, with some imagination.

This guy named Dante gave Hell a face,
    which is rude & magnificent
'cause he could have just as easily
been more inspiring & written
about the Circles of Heaven.

I guess a tiered cake
of bliss is less interesting.

According to Dante, you have to travel
through nine circles of torture
& ride the genitals of the actual Devil
out of Hell.

No wonder no one leaves Hell—
    that's a steep price for joy.

(Faerry) in My AP English Class

New kid, means lots of giggling.
New kid, means lots of showing off.
Faerry sits, legs crossed under the desk.
I notice three more daisies on the base of his neck.
(Making this boy literally a garden.)
His soft gray eyes find me. Find me inspecting him.
I whisper, *Tight desk when you have wings.*
He winks. *You want to see my wings, Whimsy?*

Teacher Questions for New Kid?

Teacher: *Where are you from, Faerry?*
How was your last school?
What's your favorite book?

Your parents are senators?

Faerry: *From everywhere. Nowhere.*
A school is a school, I guess.
Whatever book I am reading.

Yes. They are.
Lots of dinner parties,
lots of smiling,
I am very good at smiling.

Faerry flashes his perfect teeth.
The class (of course) swoons.

Questions on the Reading?

Mrs. Trace asks,
Whimsy, what did you
think of the reading?

I blink looking around the room
before glancing at the clock.

I lost twenty minutes to
a thought spiral, to *whimsy.*

I lick my lips & try to clear
my throat but it comes out as a stifled
cough that makes the class start to crackle
like Pop Rocks candy hissing in my mouth.

I think one circle in particular
has her nervous, Mrs. Trace.
A boy with dark brown hair
& blue eyes glares at me.
Is that it, Whimsy?

That's enough, Kevin.
Mrs. Trace places
her hands on her hips.
We can come back to you, Whimsy.

Same kid (Kevin) snorts.
Same kid (Kevin)

who is my ex says,
But will she still be here
when we do?

I whip around.
I dunno will you
still "be here"
when I shove
this book down
your throat, Kevin?

Whimsy, that is grossly inappropriate.
Apologize. I seal my lips. *Whimsy?*

A joke about that sort of thing is a threat.
Faerry rolls a pencil between his fingers.
I think any therapist would agree.

I'm fine, Faerry.
I don't need his help.
I don't need anyone's help.
Hush, or I'll shove a book
down your throat next.

Faerry's lip inches up.
I promise not to bite.

Get your things, Whimsy.
Go to the principal's office.

Mrs. Trace's face turns
candy apple red.
Now!

I gather
my things as everyone giggles
sounds like
spilt Skittles.

Circles of Hell

How can you condemn someone
to the seventh circle of a place
in your made-up world?

Inferno has a tier of Hell for Suicides
which is horrible & should be illegal because
a mind is still a mind without endorphins.

There are ripples in depression.
It's not all or nothing.
It's not their fault.

It's not.
It's not.
My fault.

Faerry Gathers His Things Too

The giggles stop skittling.

What are you doing, Faerry?
Mrs. Trace frowns at Faerry.
I frown at Faerry.

Civil disobedience.
He throws his backpack
on his shoulder, walks
to my desk to grab
my stack of books.

By the time he arrives
at the door, the entire class's mouths
are upside-down orange slices.

What?
Mrs. Trace's mouth
is caramel sticky.

Civil disobedience.
Your lack of concern for
a threat that involves mental health
worries me, so, I'm protesting.
Faerry's eyes glitter at me.

Faerry, you are not
excused from class,
Mrs. Trace yells.

My voice is unsteady.
Bullshit, you are skipping.

Faerry taps his lip,
Maybe. Maybe not.

I swallow,
Faerry leaves.
I weave through the desks
looking at the angry faces
of the girls who thought
the new kid was hot as hell
but have realized they might be too vanilla for him.
Kevin's eyes scorch me, accusing.

We leave
(a rose & a thorn)
Faerry & Whimsy
Together.

CHAPTER 4

RUNAWAY

Tea Leaves: Anchor
Usually represents loyal friendship
& sometimes love.

We Walk

Past ten classrooms.
Past the lunchroom
holding second block
lunch kids.

Past the front office
& the sign-in table
with the lady yelling at us to
    Stop.
        Stop.
            Stop.
We don't stop.
We keep going
    past the too-expensive cars
past Kevin's Lamborghini.

We stop at an older silver
BMW with black interior,
the color of penguin gummies.

Faerry unlocks the door
slides in, reaches over & pushes
the passenger door open—
    His eyebrows say,
So are you coming,
or are you going to the office?

I slide into the seat,

    the leather is cool through my jeans.

Faerry notices, swipes on the seat warmer.

I notice his black sunshades hooked

to the front of his sweater,

pulling it down, showing off

a black sunflower on his chest.

He tosses me his iPod.

    You pick.

He has a playlist called

    "Summoning Demons."

That's what I play.

Car Ride

It's raining because the sky
is angry we ditched.

My mother would say,
    Whimsy, you can't run away
from everything.

My dad would say,
    Whimsy, Whimsy, Whimsy?
The same statement in two different tongues.

I could have walked away
    I should have walked away,
not to the office,
maybe home, which is only
two miles from school.

But I am here,
    in a car with a Fae/Witch named Faerry.
I turn up the music
to keep him from talking.

It works for all of 2 minutes.

So, Inferno. Faerry's voice is soft
swirling like cotton candy. *Good book.*

I glare.
I want to glare a hole
        through his center.
I want to glare nine holes
    that get exponentially
        bigger through his center.

Faerry swallows. Seems nervous.
Seems like a real boy for a moment.
I mean good except
for the rings of torture of course.

It's fine with the rings of torture.

She speaks!
He smiles.

I spoke in class.

That's different.
You were not speaking
to only me.
    Also, now that
we are chatting,
want to get coffee?

A red light halts us.
No, Faerry.

Ok, Whimsy.
His hands tighten
on the wheel.

Thanks for the necklace,
I say quickly.

You said you wanted the moon.
He shrugs.

Where did you get it?

He swallows hard.
The locket was my sister's.
The moonstone was mine,
now yours.

She won't mind?
I fiddle with the locket.
What's her name?

Not really her style anymore,
& Tale.

I nod.
Faerry & Tale.

We Keep Driving

& suddenly coldness
claims my chest.

Panic. Panic. Panic
like in my nightmares.

It feels like branches are scraping
against my inner eye.

I look up,
we are on the road
that snakes through
a part of the Forest—
    it's hazy, the branches point at me saying,
It's your fault, Whimsy, it is all your fault.

I glue my eyelids closed.
Tell myself the trees
are just trees—
they don't move
like chess pieces
trying to trap me.

Faerry reaches over
& touches my hair.
You're shaking.
Are you ok, Whimsy?

My eyes unseal.
I count & breathe
like they taught me to
in the hospital.
Yeah. Great, Faerry. Thanks.

Faerry adjust his sunglasses
with fingernails painted
a sparkling black.

He has three piercings
(silver half-moon stud
gold hoop & obsidian stone)
decorating the ear that I can see,
I know there are more
studding the other ear.
I notice two tiny tattoos
ghosting his hairline
(a tiny skelton flower
beside a sea anemone).
I concentrate on tiny details
to keep my mind from racing.

We turn onto our street.
Are you sure you are ok?

Can we not talk for a moment?

He taps the wheel.

I swallow.

You seem uneasy.
I want to help.

Why, Faerry?

He fiddles with
a bracelet on his wrist
with a *T* on it.
Can you like
chill for one second?

Go to hell.
I hate how my
instincts trust him.

Which circle?
He snorts.

All of them.

You are delightful,
truly, Whimsy.
He laughs.

It's not funny.

He frowns.
It's not funny.

Why are you here, Faerry?
I frown back.

He clears his throat.

Maybe we could hang out . . .

No.

Ok, or not.

That's great too,

Faerry says as he pulls into my driveway.

The new book in English is going over my head.

It's Hansel & Gretel.

Fairy Tales are the hardest.

Don't you think? Faerry reaches over

& plucks a stray hair from my sweater.

That's the thing, Faerry.

I try not to think,

I say, thinking of the Forest.

Helps with the entire dark abyss thing.

Whimsy, I just feel

like I know you, ok.

Well, you don't!

I climb out of the car.

Right, which is why I said

I feel like I know you.

He tilts his head. *Details are important.*

I stare at my feet outside the car.
Feeling slightly bad for being rude.
By the way, are you ok?
This morning, I overheard . . .

I am fine.
I am great.
Stellar. I love when people
spy on my pain.

We are both so good at lying.
I slam the car door
annoyed again.

Faerry rolls down the window
& yells, *Almost like we invented it.*

Home

No one is home,
but my pills (vitamins this time)
are on the unicorn napkin
because Mom read that vitamin D
helps with depression.

I go upstairs
to think
think
think
about anything but the Forest & the Garden.

Still, vines seem to lace
with my fingers.

I slam my pillow against the wall,
it hits a picture frame holding
a boy with black coiled hair
round almond-brown eyes
& deep brown skin.
(Cole).

Cole,
my best friend, my brother—
who my parents say went missing
10 years ago . . .
I remember different.

Cole Is Missing?

That is how my parents recall it—
    like any moment
he could walk through the front door
    like a miracle.

Like any moment he could be found
& go to college, & graduate, & get married
    & fall in lust & fall in love.

I think this is exactly how my mom magicked it
except it didn't work on me—
    I am the only one in the universe
who remembers (most) of the truth,
but even that is sometimes hazy—
    like sea spray coming off waves.

CHAPTER 5

THE FOREST WITH THE GARDEN

Tea Leaves: Arrow
Unpleasant news is coming,
generally, from the direction
the arrow is pointing.
If there are many arrows
pointing in many directions—
hide.

Consequences at Dinner

Of course, the school called—

because of our civil disobedience.

Of course, I am suspended

for October 30 & 31

(along with Faerry)

who my mother says

Is a bad influence you should

not associate with.

She says, *I called his parents,*

they said he is rough around the edges.

She says it like she knows him.

Of course, we have a talk.

Of course, they are worried

I might melt down

into chocolate soup again.

We are saying this

because we love you, Whimsy.

Mom hugs me.

I know. I'm sorry.

Can't you see

that I'm trying?

& if I was a wooden boy,

my nose would grow.

I go up to my room,
it really doesn't matter.
I'm suspended for 2 days.

On October 31, I sit in silence, anyway,
I keep my sweet tongue to myself.
I made it this way, 10 years ago
when, according to Mom & Dad, Cole vanished.

Sometimes silence grows
thick as foxgloves covering
the ground & I think,
Maybe I can create a new day with quietness.
If I am silent enough, silence
might become a soft blanket
for Cole to land on.

I am always wishing for
October 32,
& everyone else
is stepping
forward.
Moving forward.
Racing forward
into November.

After 10 p.m. There Is a Knock

At the door & a police officer shuffles in saying,
Faerry's parents reported him missing.
Do you know where he is?

No. I swallow.

The school says you & Faerry left school early.
The officer scribbles on his notepad.
Did you get into any trouble?

No. I fold my arms.
Faerry just dropped
me off.

Can anyone confirm that?
The officer clicks his tongue,
like a snapdragon flower.
I see you both have a very long record of skipping,
& breaking the rules.

I glare.

See, we must investigate these things,
& then there are the neighbors who claim
you hang dolls in the Forest at the end
of the lane & curse people.

That's not true.
I frown.
I never go into the Forest.

Mom steps in. *Whimsy only goes near the edge of the Forest. What exactly are you claiming?*

The officer coughs. Swallows.
Listen, I am just trying to do my job.
He pulls a book, *Hansel & Gretel*, from his pocket.
We found this on the edge. It has your name in it.

My mouth unseals.
I must have left it in the car.

The officer frowns.
Then how did it get on the edge of the Forest?
I don't know.
I worry Faerry went in.

Mom steps in front of me.
You need to leave, now.

The officer says something
about coming back,
I know Mom's magic
will stop that from happening.

I am just wondering
where (in hell) is Faerry.

Things I Did Not Tell the Officer

1. Faerry is magic.
2. You won't be back, Mom conjured a forgetting spell.
3. Mom has tried forgetting spells on me.
4. But I never forget everything. I remember sharp fragments.
5. The Forest is not what it seems (anymore).
6. When sorrow eats at the roots of things, they change.
7. I have not been in the Forest for 10 years.
8. Faerry is afraid of Forests too.
9. Faerry doesn't know how dangerous Haunting Forest is.
10. Not all Gardens are beautiful.
11. At the center of the Forest there is no start or end.

October 30

Faerry is still missing,
he left everything behind
(phone & wallet).
It is like he flew into the sky.
Or sank into the ground
or got lost without bread crumbs
in the Forest.

October 30 (Midday)

I know he is in the Forest,

    he doesn't know that the only way out is through.

October 30 (Nighttime)

I think I feel him

        in the Forest tangled

in the weeds, somewhere past

the clearing, perhaps inside

a candy house.

Tiny bits of memory race back

        to me . . . the parts I did forget.

October 31

I live in silence
for Cole.
(Gone for years now.)

I live in silence
for Faerry.
(Gone more than a day now.)

I live in silence
for joy.
(Missing in action.)

I live in silence
for magic.
(Ancestors always close.)

I live in silence
for the hurt.
(Knifing at my ribs.)

I live
still,
(somehow)
but
in
silence.

Evening: October 31
(Of My 18th Year)

Doorbell rings.

Parents are at a Halloween party
thankfully, because bad influence's parents are here.

Faerry's Mom (Isolde): *Here's the thing,*
I think you know something.

Whimsy: *Says the person who sent*
the police here.

Faerry's Dad (Tristan): *I checked the edge of the Forest,*
it is filled with your pain. He won't make it out of it.
You Conjurers make it dangerous for all of us.

Whimsy: *I told him not to go in.*

Faerry's Mom: *Hoodoo tears watered those trees*
& now they are haunted for all magical beings.
It is your fault.

Whimsy: *I was 8 years old.*
I was 8 years old.

Faerry's Mom (steps too close): *Whimsy,*
you know you can fix the Forest by going all the way
through it. Witches know this, Conjurers know this.

Whimsy: *I can't.*

Faerry's Dad: *Weak Conjurers.*

Whimsy: *Weak? You don't even*
get your son help.
He came to the hospital alone.

Faerry's Dad: *Nothing is wrong*
with our son.

Whimsy: *I think he gets to decide that*
Black boys can feel
whatever they want.

Faerry's Mom (tears in her eyes):
Whimsy, our son is afraid of Forests.
He won't get out. He'll be stuck.
Forever . . . in your magic.

Whimsy: *I'll get stuck too . . .*
then what would my parents do?

Faerry's Mom: *I am begging you.*
I've already lost one child.

Whimsy: *What?*

Faerry's Mom: *My daughter, Tale,*
is missing. Missing for 10 years.

Whimsy: *Missing?*

Faerry's Dad: *We have searched everywhere.*

Whimsy: *Oh my god,*
I say with memories
stacking weight on my chest.

Faerry's Mom:
We know you have been through a lot . . .

Whimsy: *I can't help.*
I am sorry.

I slam the door.
I can't
I can't
go back into the Forest,
I'll never get out,
a second time.

CHAPTER 6

WHAT I REMEMBER

Tea Leaves: Dragon
Can signal a sudden change
that will most likely be dangerous.

Haunting Forest

Did you know that trees talk?
    Scientifically another tree can
send love to a sad one, or a sick one.

Baby trees hardly get any light—
    which means every baby tree should die,
but the roots of the vast trees feed it.

Some forests are just fine.
They are roots & love & joy
& babbling brooks.

Did you know if something
poisons one tree,
    the forest can suffer.

That's how I think it happened—
    that's why all this is my fault.

I cried my enchanted sorrow away at the base
of a water beech (130 ft tall & 6 ft wide).
I watered it well with my glittering pain
& the branches snapped & the bark fell
    as I scrambled away—
& suddenly instead of a water beech,

there was a candy house in the middle
of the Garden—
    the Forest whispered,
The only way out is through, Whimsy.

Then the Garden came to eat—
    my sugar-rotten soul.

Finding Cole

This is how my parents remember it:
When Cole "disappeared," Mom & Dad tried everything—
 the police came & searched every inch of the Forest.
They said they found a scarf dangling from a water beech tree
& nothing else.

They said they found no footprints except mine.

They questioned me—
all I knew is I cried & cried & told them
the truth—it was all my fault—
 Cole was not missing he was gone, dead, gone.

The police said, *The evidence does not*
align with your truth.

In a month, the police called the case cold.

Mom & Dad hired a private investigator,
after a year of Mom & Dad crying
 they decided we had to say *goodbye,*
adios, au revoir.

Except, sometimes I don't remember that they searched,
 sometimes I wonder if that happened.

I do know that no amount of searching—
 can resurrect the dead.

This Is What I Remember

I was so sad the day of the *Goodbye Ceremony* (that is what Mom & Dad called it) & the hugging trees felt like a blanket. I ran into the Garden & everything was normal. The tiny blue bottles of water (hung by me & Cole for protection) swung in the breeze. It was all fine, until I saw the water beech tree & the tears came strong & fast. Until a gust of wind, blue & icy, swept them from my face & my tears mingled with Oreo soil & the water beech tree melted its skeletal fingers like dark boiling chocolate & reappeared as a candy house.

The Candy House

I called for Cole,
but no one answered
& I knew if he was missing
in the Forest he would have
run, sprinted, raced
to save me.

There were other new things
in the Forest too, stones sticking up
from the ground, numbered to nine.

Still, I stayed (because I wanted
the Forest to hug me).

I watched the water beech
that turned into a candy house,
wringing my laced black gloves.

The house dripped sweets & chocolate.
Giant gumdrop shrubs surrounded it.

I was so hungry, so empty . . .
I followed the path of mirror
glaze to an (open) licorice-rimmed entry.

Mist seeped out the door
into the air & the leaves

of surrounding trees crumpled—
dead, dying, gone.

I stepped in,
tired, not having anywhere else to go.
    So often there is nowhere else to go.

Inside the Candy House

The house was empty
except things floated
around in it of their own accord
like invisible haunts were carrying
things in their invisible hands
but I just could not see them.

On the wooden table in front of me
a piece of coal sat on top of a Fairy Tale notebook
that had a red thorned rose in its pages.

Sit. Stay a while,
a voice without a body said.
So, I sat because I was tired.

Some time passed.
I *think* I remember someone banging
on the mirror glass windows
of the candy house.

I think I remember two baby owls
(one gray, one white)
slipping in through the cracked window.

I am sure I remember
the velvet voice
without a body

saying, *You live here now,*
have some chocolate.

The chocolate tasted delicious
for a moment,
because I was hungry.
Then a weighty cloud
came to sit on my chest
with bone-breaking speed.

Here, have another piece.
I am only trying to help,
Dearest Whimsy.
& my 8-year-old brain
remembered things . . .
sad things, hard things . . .

A boy called me "*Blackie*"
spat at me & tugged my hair.
I covered my 8-year-old face,
collapsing to the candy floor yelling,
Cole. Cole. Cole. Help.

No one is coming to help you . . .
the bodyless voice snickered.

I tucked myself so far into myself
I could not move or breathe.

I remember a window smashing, & hooting,
tiny running steps, silver feathers
& a voice saying—
The only way out is through.

I remember it was my fault
& then there is nothing.

The Clearing

Next, I recall,
Dad found me in the clearing,
curled up with frost
like powdered sugar
clinging to my curly licorice hair
with a new pair of too-big moonstone
shoes stuffed with feathers on my feet
& the outline, but no body,
of another form beside me
a form that appeared
to have delicate wings.

Mom put me in a warm bath saying,
Looks like a hawk or an eagle
was watching over you.

I tried to explain.
I tried to tell them not to go into the Forest,
that there was a haunted Garden at the center.

Whimsy, go to sleep, darling,
Mom said as she wove magic.

Trying to melt the bad memories,
(in her way) trying to manage sadness
& dissolve it like sugar in water.

I closed my eyes.
Mom & Dad thought I was asleep & I heard her say,
I am taking our memories next & theirs too.
So, we all have a chance to smile again—
To start over. It's all our fault.
Only problem is,
I was the only one who did not all-the-way forget—
I pretend the memories are gone,
but (it hurts so much).

Now, I am the reason
no one gets to smile again.

CHAPTER 7

PINKY PROMISE

Tea Leaves: Broom
Changes are coming into your life.

The Edge

10:50 p.m. & I sit on the edge of my bed,
    my altar bright from the moon,
something glows, sitting under a moonstone.

A silver feather, with a note—
        Don't come for me, Whimsy.
            It's hard, my parents don't get it.
                I am cracking. Like a tree hit by lightning.
                    I want to rest, in the Forest—I am guilty.

The feather is warm in my hand.
I grab my backpack (with the phases
of the moon down the center).

I stuff crystals, a blanket,
        herbs & my Fairy Tale notebook inside.
I take the stairs (two at a time)—
because I promised him
I wouldn't let the Forest get him,
because his wings remind me
of the moon.

Because the Forest eats the guilty
& I think (maybe) Faerry & I
are both guilty (somehow).

In Haunting Forest Again

At first, it's ok. I drop bread crumbs
to find my way out, because sometimes
the trees shift like oak chess pieces,
but the bread crumbs I dropped
grew into headstones—

I take a coin from my pocket,
& drop it to the ground.

It sizzles & pops like a pancake
on a skillet—
making it clear
this time nothing
will mark my way out.
    The only way is forward.

A chill wind whistles & I see it (the candy house)
where the water beech tree used to be
where I cried a tiny pond of magic tears.

I squint & see Faerry
in the window
banging
trapped
trapped.
    So small,
        in the window.

Blood drips down his
wrist as he tries to break
the candy windows
but not faster than
they are reglazed.

Whimsy in Sorrow's Garden

Behind me, snakes spill from the Forest rainbow- &
gummy-like—hissing & snapping. The dirt under my feet shifts,
creeping with thousands of earthworms bubbling to the surface
like they are trying to escape some sort of danger rooted in the
moist soil.

They stick to my shoes, try to climb up my pant legs & I shake
them off & jump the candy fence & venture toward peppermint
stairs. Behind me the snakes hiss outside the gate, begging me
to come to them, with them away from Faerry. *Leave your friend
behind,* they say. *We will be your friend,* they promise. *We will build
you a lovely house—here.*

The snakes don't cross the dipped-chocolate fence
of the candy house. Worms don't wiggle
in the soil inside the barrier of the green fence.
I swallow, glaring at the door
that even the snakes are afraid of. Even the worms don't go near
the ghost (called Sorrow),
with only a voice, which lives inside the candy house.

The House Sorrow Built

I move from the door & use my sleeve
to wipe away the powdered sugar
clouding the picture window.
I cup my hands around my face like a bowl
to peer into the candy house where Sorrow lives. I see Faerry—
on his knees, panting—hands covering his ears, trying to un-hear
a voice I know well.

I bang on the glass, trying to get his attention,
but he doesn't hear me
begging him, *Look at me*. Then I see *it*, Sorrow isn't just a voice
(it has a body now). Dressed in blue, sitting at the
head of the table,
laughing, laughing, laughing at me outside the window, it says—
Look how the tables have turned,
as always, the only way out is through.

& the door to the candy house opens gently,
inviting me into hell, gently.
Asking me to stay, gently.

No one ever tells you that Sorrow doesn't grab you by the throat.
It opens the door, offers a warm fire, says—*Have some candy.*

& I step inside (again).

Meeting Sorrow Again

Faerry sees me in the doorway,
he raises his head & arches
an eyebrow as if to say,
    I said leave me,
        can you read?

I grind my jaw
as if to say,
Sounded more like
here is a dramatic note
save me, save me.

Faerry's frown
is like wrinkled foil,
new lines river it.

Sorrow's eyes find mine,
& I turn into an ice pop
frozen to the core.

Whimsy. I've felt you
at the edge of my Forest.
Sorrow rasps, *As you can see,*
    I've grown. I've got a body now.

When the door slams
I flinch but keep

my voice steady.
Give him back.
We are not staying.

Sorrow stands its icy ground.
You won't escape this time.
This time you're (both) mine.

I grab my head
& an ache grows
at the center
of my brain,
like ice
fracturing.
What are you doing?

Then Sorrow is on me.
Remember me, Whimsy.
Remember it all.

Sorrow tugs me
closer, its hands
laced with maggots
& so cold they feel
as hot as the center
of a flame.

The Only Way

Sorrow has me by the neck (again).

Faerry hurls a jar of jelly beans
at it. *Let Whimsy go! I came here,*
take me.

Sorrow's grip stays firm.
That's what she said last time,
"Let Faerry go, I came here, take me."
Remember, Faerry . . .
Do you remember?

Faerry's face changes, like he just recalled
something he forgot—
We've been here before?

Faerry stands taller & magicks something white & fluffy from
his mouth into the flames that still lap & lick from the hearth
but feel cool like a fall breeze moving through crisp leaves.

The frosted picture window to the candy house shatters
& two owls swoop in pecking & snapping at Sorrow
that releases my neck (now marked with its fingerprints).
I land on the floor with a thump. Faerry grabs me, says,
Go through the fire,
trust me.

I lace my fingers with his because fire & burning
are safer when I'm laced to Faerry.

The only way out is through,
I say as we leap
into the flames
away from Sorrow.

& we fall
    fall
fall into the Garden
together—
undoing the stitches
re-stitching memories
like we fall into
a different dimension
where Mom's magic
doesn't stick at all.

& I *remember* Faerry
I *remember* we've been here
(in the Garden) together before.

Abandon All Hope

In the Garden Sorrow Built

How is it
that falling
(sometimes) feels like flying?

(Sometimes)
feels
like
soaring.

Until we
(Whimsy & Faerry)
hit the
ground.

& pain
knocks us
back to life.

Enter Here

Faerry & I roll to our knees
then stand on our feet
grass & trees surround us.

Faerry points at my neck.
Sorrow left its fingerprints on you.

It always does,
doesn't it?

Faerry grabs my hand & nods toward
a giant vined archway that resembles wrought iron.
The vines wind into different shapes (skulls, spiders, knives)
& in the arch at the top is a sign,
spiked poisonous vines—
ABANDON ALL HOPE
ALL WHO ENTER SORROW'S GARDEN.

Faerry holds my hand tighter.

Do you remember?
I ask.

We were friends. We were 8, you got lost in the Forest,
I ran after you . . . because we were guilty.
Faerry exhales slowly.
The Forest is different this time,
Sorrow isn't just a voice this time,
Sorrow has a face this time.

I think it's 'cause we have
lived with Sorrow now. It has grown.
I touch Faerry's cheek.
You look frightened.

I am.
He swallows.
I am always so frightened
of forgetting, of my own hands.

I am frightened too,
I confess.

Should we turn back?
Or maybe we could just stay here.

My spirit falters.
We can only go forward.
Remember?

Together.
Faerry faces the vined archway.
Hello, Sorrow.

Always together.
I tighten my rib cage—armor ready.
Bonjour, Sorrow.

This time the Garden is darker,
older, wittier than when

we entered it 10 years ago—
& living has beaten us both raw.

We enter through the archway
together (again).

Hope Sinks

We walk & haze quickly makes our vision blurry, it thickens
& we see nothing—not even the leaves of the giant trees.

I can't see anything,
I say, feeling my way.

Faerry's hand holds mine firmly.
We don't have to see the path,
we just have to keep putting
one foot in front of the other.

We walk & it could be forward or backward,
but we keep walking—
each step feels like our hope (that once lived high in our chests)
sinks deep into the arches of our feet.
A hooting warning echoes through the trees.
I think something is coming.
I spin around, listening closely.
We stop walking. The haze slowly lifts & the Garden
appears again. Lush & strange & silent. We are in a clearing
& something is not right.

My body feels light,
halfway gone
like a dandelion seed.

Beside me Faerry's feet
crunch the leaves
like a giant.

Me (weightless)
    Faerry (heavy as stone)—
like I might fly away & he might sink
    down, down, down—
deep into the worm-filled ground.

I swallow.
I think this
is the first test.

Faerry strains
to lift his leg.
If I remember right
this is already
harder than before.

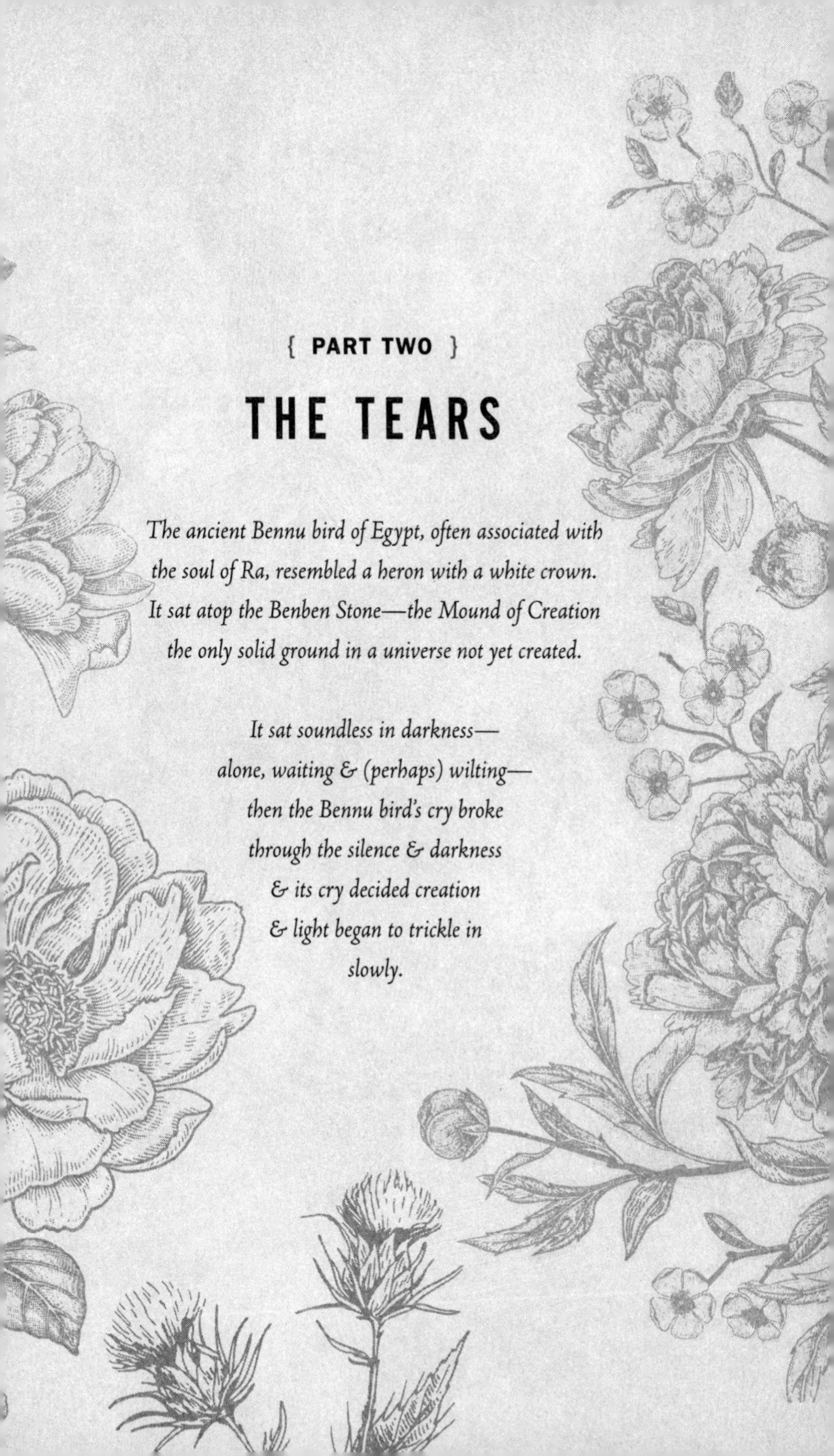

{ **PART TWO** }

THE TEARS

The ancient Bennu bird of Egypt, often associated with the soul of Ra, resembled a heron with a white crown. It sat atop the Benben Stone—the Mound of Creation the only solid ground in a universe not yet created.

It sat soundless in darkness—
alone, waiting & (perhaps) wilting—
then the Bennu bird's cry broke
through the silence & darkness
& its cry decided creation
& light began to trickle in
slowly.

CHAPTER 8

BABA YAGA'S HOUSE

11:02 PM

Angelica Root: Hoodoo
Also known as the Holy Ghost Root,
often used for protection.

(My Sorrow Garden)

The trees are haunted
bending at the hip
closing in, scratching us.

Faerry's feet sink
into the sticky soil
like caramel quicksand.
I feel so heavy,
like there are bricks
in my pockets.

I reach under Faerry's arms
trying to keep him from sinking.
You have to keep standing, Faerry.

Above us two wise owls circle,
hooting & flapping
(one gray, one white)
their wings frantically—
begging us to pay attention.

Fog, heavy & thick & gray
crawls from the forest toward us.
The tendrils look like ghost arms
(rotting & stinking) reaching stretching—
coming for us.

Faerry's fingers find mine
& twine, our pulses match.

This fog is in my Fairy Tale notebook,
I say with wide eyes.

What does it do, in your notebook?
Faerry says, clinging to my hand tighter,
my nails tattoo half-moons
in the center of his palm.

It traps you in cloudy memories forever.
With my free hand I grab
blessed dirt from my backpack
for foot-magic (Hoodoo work).
We can't get stuck in it.

We slowly back away, while I sprinkle
blessed dirt in front of us (to protect our way,
to slow the fog down & because that is what
Grandmother taught me).
The faceless fog pauses then grows
upward taller, taller, taller,
like an infinite beanstalk—
then it comes for us,
a gray ghostly wall.

Run, Whimsy.
Faerry squeezes my hand

& we try to outrun the fog,
the sadness, the sorrow,
that is always coming for us.

We run (hand in hand).
We don't stop.

Until Faerry trips & Faerry's fingers slip from mine,
& I turn to find a hole in the ground
& I worry he has fallen all the way
down into the depths of hell.

No! I scream.
No! I yell,
reaching my hand
down into the hole
filled with thousands
of wiggling earthworms.

The opening shrinks
around my arm, closes.

No matter how much
I grasp, I only grab dirt
filled with earthworms.

Faerry is gone,
gone,
gone.

(When It Rains Ice)

The fog still comes. I drop the dirt gorged with worms
  & run as rain pelts me cold as slush.

My lungs ask for air but all I inhale is ice.
  So much ice I think my heart might freeze.

My lips are cracked & blue. My fingers are numb.
  Panic ripples like doom coming for me.

I slip. My head bangs the ground, hard.
  I look up through teary eyes & see another house.

This one is not made of candy. It's familiar,
down to the blue shutters & white trim.

It's my safe place (Grandma's house).
Just like the one I described in my Fairy Tale notebook.
Same blue porch covered
   in leaves,
     leaves,
       leaves.

(Sorrow & Memories)

I swallow, looking at the house that reminds me of Grandma.
The Garden has gotten crafty, mixing my memories & sorrow—
    taking the Fairy Tales from my notebook & hammering them
into something completely different.

I stand, remembering Grandma.
My grandma used to leave food out at night,
fried chicken on the counter, cookies by the TV
& black-eyed peas for New Year's.
She claimed,
        The past can be fed & made different,
                gentleness can change things.

I scale the stairs & remember how Grandma said,
Magic & sorrow are real, Whimsy, & both have endless possibilities.

I wonder what in hell waits for me in the house—
(that looks like Grandma's suburban home)
    in the middle of the Garden crafted
    from (Faerry's & my) tears—
                    & I open the door.

(Grandma's Twin House in the Garden)

The house is acquainted with emptiness. So unlike Grandma's house in real life. Cobwebs drape over the table set for ten. Food is out rotting & oozing. In the front window, lace drapes & a solitary spider large & red, lonely & webbing. I stumble out of the small kitchen where I used to sit listening to Grandma sing "His Eye Is on the Sparrow" to me & Cole as we drew flowers & Grandma taught us their names. It's like Grandma's house & not, Grandma's house never felt un-lived in.

The floors groan, cradling my steps, waltzing with all my heaviness, asking if I might stay here, love here, live here forever. I follow the stairs to the cellar, where Christmas decorations stay up all year long—everything is as I remember (except for) a tiny, hatched door in the middle of the floor with stairs leading to a second, deeper cellar. I climb down the steeper stairs & arrive at Grandma's front door, again—feeling heavy, heavy, heavy—like metal is in my bones.

I open the front door (again) & this time it's darker & the rot from the food now smells like a dumpster & more cobwebs drape like cotton candy over everything.

I think, *I am stuck,*
if I go through the cellar again,
I might end up somewhere deeper.

My grandma used to say,
Most things die waiting for something
but in Hoodoo we don't wait
we create.

After Grandma died & Cole was gone—I used to wait for laughter in silence until I forgot its sound.

In my head I hear Grandma say,
You're a Conjurer, Whimsy.
That comes with responsibility.
&, my dear, you will suffer more than many.
& your magic might trap you,
but remember the way out is through.

I swallow hard.
I don't know the way out.
How do I get out?

(Meeting Baba Yaga)

A rocking chair pushes against the wooden floors.
I whip around to find an old woman (I don't know who)
rocking back & forth in a chair.
You have spirit, child,
but that won't save you from your memories,
from sorrow—
trust me. I know.

Who are you?
I ask, breathless.
Is this your Garden?
Why does this look like
my grandma's house?

Stories call me Baba Yaga.
Girl, this is yours, you crafted all of this,
from that notebook in your backpack.
Your magic brought me here.

My magic is not that strong,
I say.

The Garden would disagree.
We are both here, are we not?
She taps her nose. *I am still here*
because of my own sadness—
I am too sorrow-filled to travel through.

I swallow,
remembering the stories
I wrote about Baba Yaga
(metal nose, hates boys, powerful witch).
You've been so sad, you cried a puddle too?

Who hasn't been sad enough to cry a puddle, girl?
Baba Yaga's metal nose sniffs the air.
You brought a boy with you?
She sniffs again. *I don't like boys.*

I lost him. He sank into the ground.
My voice breaks.
I am always losing things.

Baba Yaga gets up, comes so close
her metal nose almost touches mine—
You're a Conjurer?

Yes.

You didn't lose him, child.
Your magic, your Hoodoo & blessed dirt
sent him out, to the edge of your Garden.
Question now is:
Will the boy stay out of the Garden,
or come back for you?

I touch the locket.
Oh, no. He'll come back.
Don't come back, Faerry.

Baba Yaga snickers.

& hobbles back to her rocking chair.

Wouldn't put too much faith in that, child.
Men & boys are very disappointing.

I swallow.
Help me?
How do I get out?

Listen, girl, I don't have any magic left
to help you. But I'll lead you
in the right direction.
The rest is up to you.

She fills a red bag
with angelica root & rosemary,
& chants over it.

If you make it through, we are all free
to roam wherever we like (again).

How many people are there in the Garden?
I wet my lips.

How many did you write,
in that Fairy Tale notebook?

I nod slowly.
Many.

This is a bit of angelica root.
Baba Yaga taps my head.
Add more flowers from the Garden
to the bag. Flowers from all the Fairy Tales
you wrote. Now, all you have to do
is open the front door, barefoot, feel the dirt
& take the first step. The most important step.
I will make it through,
I say, removing my shoes.
I will make it through, Baba Yaga,
I say, hand hovering over the doorknob.
Baba Yaga's eyes light up.
Fierceness becomes you, Whimsy.

(Outside Baba Yaga's House)

I step out of the house my magic built
curls dancing with magic, barefoot, my backpack
filled with herbs & my hands filled with magic.

It feels like I have stepped out of this house before
but with fewer tools—no backpack, no angelica root.

My toes sink into the ground, legs like tree trunks,
& I wait for what happens next.
I wait while my legs shake
& the fog climbs toward me.

My toes dig into the soil, I feel strength rise up my spine.
I won't look away. I won't back down.
If I go back into Baba Yaga's house, I have a feeling
the way out will disappear.

I'll be stuck there forever & ever.

CHAPTER 9

ESCAPING SORROW (AGAIN)

11:03 PM

Honeysuckle:
An edible yellow flower
with a sweet taste,
some can be poisonous.

(Back at the Start)

The fog engulfs me, pushes smoke down my throat
& just when I think I'll choke forever, the fog
slams me to the ground, pebbles embedded in my palms
as I try to stand.

It looks like I am back at the start.
Sorrow's candy house stands sweetly
in front of me.

I tighten my backpack straps
slip my shoes back on
pull on my leather gloves
& exhale counting to ten—
    just like my therapist taught me.

I open the gate, scale the stairs
& look through the picture window—
air races out of my lungs.

I see Faerry is shirtless,
his garden of tattoos bright
& stunning, but tiny cuts
oozing strawberry blood
crisscross his skin.

I kick in the door.
Don't touch him!

I run to Faerry,
covered in cuts.
Why did you come back?
Baba Yaga said I got you out
of my Garden.
You shouldn't have come back.

Faerry smiles weakly.
I could never leave you
alone in this sorrow, Whimsy.

Sorrow waits,
heels on its wooden table
next to a vase of honeysuckles.

Realization dawns on me.
I whisper to Faerry,
We need those flowers.
That is why we are here again.

Sorrow drags its fingers slowly
through peppered
gray smoke hair saying,
Silly,
stupid.
Selfish
girl, I didn't do a thing to Faerry,
those scars are old.

I look at the marks on Faerry
as thin as razor-blade edges.
Oh, Faerry.

I used to think that is where
the pain got out.
Faerry coughs.
I don't think that anymore.

Sorrow chuckles.
Doesn't much matter when you did them,
they reopen around me. How's it feel?

I stand up & stare Sorrow down.
Leave him alone. NOW!

How about, no.
Sorrow has an ancient voice,
like cicadas & sugar.

Faerry winces
as a new cut opens (again).
Sorrow doesn't even
have to touch us
to hurt us.

I rip my shirt & try to hold it
to a cut, but there are so many.
It's ok. It's going to be ok, Faerry.

Sorrow taps its fingers.

You can't beat me.

You deserve to suffer.

Your turn now, you wanted to die once,

stupid girl, die here.

Sorrow points to the list I made

On the table:

WAYS TO MAKE AIR LEAVE MY LUNGS.

A pill bottle sits on top of it.

Sorrow smiles with rotten teeth.

May I suggest number 3 on your list (pills).

Panic makes sweat

drip down my neck.

No.

You're wrong.

Sorrow stands.

You're the reason Cole is gone.

Have you forgotten—

it's all your fault.

Remember I told you,

it's all your fault.

I was only 8 years old,

I say, fists clenched.

I ran to get help.

Sorrow towers over me.
Is that what your therapist tells you?
It's not your fault? It's always your fault, Whimsy.

I . . . I . . . I,
I say, my breath
coming out colder.

Sorrow picks up the pills.
You're the reason your brother (Cole)
& Faerry's sister (Tale) are not just missing—
they are dead.

(I Deserve the Garden)

Tangled memories
I can no longer hold in my belly
rush up my throat to my mind.

All the guilt is mine
mine
mine.

Faerry yells,
No. Whimsy.
It's not your fault.
It's mine,
mine too.
I was there too.

Sorrow presses a sharp object
into Faerry's hand & says,
That's right, it's your fault too.

(Hooting & Breaking)

Sorrow sits back at its table
& Faerry & I watch each other,
him with a sharp object hovering
over skin, me with ten pills
cupped in my shaking hand.

Tears river down both our faces.
Faerry says, *Hello, this is me.*
Guilty & covered in scars.

I swallow a sob.
Bonjour, Faerry.
This is me, thinking
of closing my eyes forever.

The sharp object hits the ground.
Hola, Whimsy, please drop the pills.

My hand only grasps them tighter.
It's different. Everything feels too much.

Sorrow sips some wine.
That is because it is; take them, Whimsy.

Outside something pecks, softly at first
then louder & louder. Sorrow stands
to open the door. *Perhaps more visitors?*

When the door opens, two large owls
swoop in. The gray one goes straight for Sorrow
pecking at its eyes. The white snowy one grabs
the honeysuckle with its beak,
lands on my shoulder & drops it in my hand.

I look into the owl's eyes,
begging me to keep going,
asking me to drop the pills.

I remember, Grandma used to say,
Owls appear when we are helpless,
    they lead us when we can't see.
That's how I wrote them in my Fairy Tale notebook.

I drop them,
they scatter like marbles.

Faerry runs to me
gathers me in his arms.
We have to go through
the fire, he says,
magicking it cool again.

Sorrow screams over the owl attack,
You think you can save each other again?

You are both much too bruised now.
Battered from life.
You belong to me.

(Through the Fire Again)

I stuff the honeysuckle in my bag.
No one is getting left behind.
We are (both) getting out—
guilty or not.

I grab Faerry's arm
& haul it over my shoulder.
He is weak, still riddled with cuts.

Then we hobble to the hearth
& fall
fall
fall &
break & break & break (again).

I try to trust the falling,
I try to forget all the things I've left behind.
I try to forget the kids I left
in the hospital,
my brother I left (by living).
My mother & father
I left (by wanting to die).

& I remember Faerry
(a memory Mom erased
with a Hoodoo spell)
picking yellow honeysuckles.

My childhood best friend—
if he was the sun, I was the moon.

I remember our older siblings (Tale & Cole)
also best friends, joined at the hip—
        Gone, missing, gone (together).

Faerry is (still) the saddest sun,
        I am (still) the sorrowful moon.

(Faerry Grabs My Hand)

I hit the ground
hard & curl in like a question mark
cradling the red flannel bag holding
roots & rosemary & honeysuckle plants.

I hear another
body hit the ground.

I crawl to Faerry, who gathers me
like a present.
I remember more now.

You were my best friend.
Tears thunder from my eyes.
Sizzling when they hit
the soil. Feeding Sorrow's Garden.
Our siblings,
Tale & Cole, were best friends.

I knew, I knew you.
Faerry wipes my tears away.

Mom took our memories, with magic.
That's why your family doesn't remember.
I am so sorry she took the truth from you,
I say, holding Faerry's hands.

She must have thought
the truth was too much.
Faerry squeezes my hand.

How did we get out before?
I say with fire kindling
my voice.

He holds me tight.
I don't know.
I can't remember that part.

I stand.
So, we are writing
our own Fairy Tale then?

Faerry nods.
We destroy the villains.

& save all the flowers.

CHAPTER 10

ANANSI
THE SPIDER'S DEN

11:04 PM

Creeping Thistle:
Has a rough exterior
because it is strong,
aggressive & protective
of what it holds.

(The Webs of Anansi)

We stand, dusting the ash off our clothes,
in front of us is a giant windmill
at least 50 feet tall, attached to an oak tree.

A thin river cuts through the soil beneath
the windmill that is blanketed in cobwebs
& speckled with the bodies of insects.

That river seems too small
for that windmill, don't you think?
I say, looking up, up, up.

It's strange how it is attached
to an oak tree, Faerry agrees.

We turn to leave but the windmill creeks
& a giant hairy leg, followed by seven more,
creeps from behind the windmill.

Did I ever mention,
I don't like spiders?
Faerry stumbles back
stepping on my foot.

Time to face your fear?
I swallow.

The spider is large
& red & shifting
with eight eyes & thistle
creeping up her legs
purple & thorny.

It has been some time
since something alive
has visited me.
She clicks.
I am Anansi.

My fingers tingle,
venom bubbles
in the air.
Hi?

Anansi?
Faerry approaches slowly.

The trickster in African Folklore.
My grandmother taught me about you,
I say, voice still shaking
remembering I wrote them
in my Fairy Tale notebook.

How did you get here?
Faerry asks, watching all
her eyes water at once.

I was lonely webbing.
No one believed
in me anymore.

She taps her head
with one long leg.

Then suddenly,
I was trapped here.

Do you want to leave?
I whisper into the venom air.

Yes, I want to go home.
A giant tear falls
breaking the surface
of the tiny river.

We can help you,
Faerry says, looking
up, up, up at the spider.

No one gets out
of this Garden.

I've gotten out before.
I shiver thinking
about it.

Anansi exhales deeply.
That's because it is yours.
It was smaller then—
you are both older now,
you've collected more Fairy Tales.
More is required.

Please help us,
Faerry says, running
his hand through is
mint-green hair.

I can't help. Sorrow has sucked
me dry, but I can offer you a riddle.
That's the way out,
answer correctly.

We're kinda in a hurry . . . ,
Faerry starts before
Anansi stomps her giant leg.

I like riddles,
I say because

it's true. I do.
Grandma told
me a few.

(Anansi Cries)

One giant tear falls, we hop away from it.

You have to answer the riddle.

Or you stay here with me.

Forever & Fairy-Tale-ever. Another giant tear falls

& the river grows wider & golden.

Please know the answer,

I want to go home.

Home.

Across the ocean home.

She extends her long legs & begins,

Is a leaf still a leaf when it's crushed & decomposing?

Is a mind still a mind if it tilts toward shadow?

When the rain falls, is it concerned that it might water the weed?

You see, you see
when a story stops being told,
when the news no longer televises,
when the false memory thinks it is true
is it still, in fact, truth?

Does a Garden crafted in magic & sorrow
have an entrance
or an exit?

(Faerry & I Discuss)

Faerry: *Everything has a beginning*
& an end.

The spider raises a long leg to Faerry's eye.
Make sure you are sure
before you answer.

Whimsy: *Sorrow has no*
start or end.
Pain is still there,
in the ground,
living in the soil
eons after we're gone.

Faerry: *That would make*
the entire earth a graveyard.

As is above? Anansi rests a leg
under her chin.
Are half the stars not dead?

Faerry: *Are you saying*
there's no way out
of this Garden?

Silly boy. She smiles.
Why wouldn't there be a way out
if you have ventured out before?

(The Answer)

Whimsy: *If no one has been through*
there is no road.
You must build one—
brick by brick.

Faerry: *& the Garden is different*
each time you travel through
because you carry different stories each time.

Whimsy: *Everything starts in the middle.*
It starts in the middle
not the beginning or the end—
stories start in the middle.

Another giant tear falls
as Anansi slams her skinny legs
on the ground & suddenly there appears
a yellow brick road.
It is also behind us now,
where our feet have landed.

Each step forward,
more yellow bricks appear.

That is exactly true.
Anansi rips a thistle
from her leg,

Keep it safe.
Remember you have risen out
of Sorrow before.
The Garden may be different
(vaster, trickier, smarter)
but your souls are magic,
you are not doing this alone.

I pull out my red flannel bag
that I keep in my shirt
over my heart.
I'll remember,
Always, I promise.

CHAPTER 11

MAMA WATA

11:05 PM

Sea Anemones:
Also known as the flowers of the sea, are actually stunning predators.

(Catching Magic)

Ahead of us,
the thin river filled
with Anansi's golden tears
hardens & hardens
& the path is shown
as a yellow brick road
that grows & grows
like yellow taffy
stretched thin,
leading us onward,
deeper into the Garden.

Faerry's eyes grow wide.
Now, that is magic.

No, Anansi cried,
that is sacrifice,
I say turning back
waving goodbye,
but meaning
hello, bonjour, hola.

She waves at us (Faerry & Me)
with six of her eight legs
& I feel six times
braver.

(Walking Memories)

We walk until our legs grow heavy so we sit
(together) me inspecting
my palms, trying to read the future
like crushed tea leaves.

Faerry studying me
like a rare crystal plucked
from the sky.

I remember,
your grandma made the best
collard greens,
Faerry says tracing my palm.

We used to charge
our parents for shoveling
the snow from the driveway.
I laugh. *Then got lots of pizza*
& watched movies.

Remember the time
we found a baby bird?

With the broken wing,
& used our allowance
to take it to the vet.
I nod, remembering
all the things
we did first together.

Our parents thought we were too close
but your grandma told them we were
twin flames—best friends forever.
Faerry exhales as I hug him.

I remember
you once showed me
your silver wings.

I did. Because I trusted you.
He frowns. *I remember the bad too . . .*
We got picked on a lot
for being Black, & smart
& different, always digging
in the dirt.

Always bullies,
but we faced them
Always together.
I pause.
How could we forget?
So many details?

Your mom's magic is strong.
Our parents don't
even remember each other.

They don't even remember
the truth. Why we are guilty . . .
We left them.

Faerry nods.
We were trying to get help.
Guilty together though, I guess.

We sit in our guilt for a long while
before we hear yelling.

Behind us, on the yellow brick road,
a gang of boys, one holding a long spider leg—
yelling *Get them, punch them, hurt them.*

I wrote these bullies this way,
        in my Fairy Tale notebook.

(Fae Wings)

Faerry grabs me & I see them (wings)
for the first time (since I was 8 years old).
Silver half-moons encase me
as the bullies descend on us
like a locust plague.

They all look different
from us (white skin
& blue eyes).

Silver
        feathers
                fly.

They rip Faerry off me,
grinding their teeth
like they want to eat us dry.

They blow dust in my eyes,
tiny diamonds, cutting my irises
& I see what they
want me to see.

Sadness, pain,
I see a fin, black skin.
A mermaid?
A girl?
Both?
I see a painful story that I wrote (in my notebook)
many years ago, coming to life.

(What I See)

I.

A girl put in a cinder-block
classroom drenched
in light, fluorescent lights,
her Blackness—inspected.

At school a girl in a green dress
white socks & shoes
with loud buckles.

Kinks pushed
out of her curly hair,
so she runs.

II.

Girl screaming,
Let me explain pain.
It reaches into your mouth,
removes what it wants,
takes your voice.

It opens your lungs
removes the air then
requests that you breathe.

A girl (with a fin)
trying to explain loneliness.

It's like a song that feathers
sing to bare skin in the hours
before dawn.

The only Black girl who knows
no one understands.
Everyone chases her,
thinks she is just a prize.

III.

A Black girl hearing
hateful words
in her green dress
& kink-less hair
so she ran with a stone
to the water.

IV.

A Black girl saying to the principal,
I'll tell you how it happened they found me,
stoned me with words, so I took a stone to the river
thought I might swim forever.

They bullied me, hung me with words—
Blackie, tar face . . .
A Black girl twisting her hands.

Why won't they stop
hanging
me?

(Back on the Yellow Brick Road)

I kick & bite & scream but still I can't escape the memory.
A rumble in the distance grows & a giant wave floods the Garden
(5 feet deep). The boys' hands hold me under, my ears pop & my eyes
add water to the flood as the boys waterfall hateful words at me.

I open my mouth to speak, but the violence chokes me—the
water chokes me. They keep holding me under, throwing hate so
hard it punches me through—bruises my brown skin. They call
me Medusa & eel hair & Blackie & they spit on me.

Under the water a different kind of garden surrounds me, filled
with coral, sea urchin & kelpy vines. Tiny fish swim toward me
(try to help) nibbling the fingers of the bullies, but they won't stop
drowning me.

I remember the coins in my pocket & manage to pull one out. I
drop it (an offering) into the water saying—

Ancestors,

Please.

Help me.

(Mama Wata & the Ocean in a Globe)

The flood ripples.
A woman with snakes
wrapped around her wrist answers.
A Conjurer.
No wonder Sorrow is frightened.
Her green fingers rest
on my heart & snakes
slither under my skin.
Be the story, child.
Be your history.

As Mama Wata speaks,
the splashing waves
stretch tall & morph
into curved walls—
    like those of a snow globe.
I am trapped. Trapped. Trapped.

I look through the glass & see Faerry
shirtless on the other side of the glass
banging against it.

Me & my assaulters
a snow globe
a fishbowl
I don't know how to shatter.

Faerry is yelling
& crying
& sobbing
& I look around him
just enough to see he is in his own glass cage,
people with red eyes throw rocks at his skin yelling—
    You shouldn't mind, you slice your own skin.

Whimsy!
he wails.
Help!

(Under the Water of Words, I Hear Them [the Bullies] Say)

1. Why is she splashing so hard?
2. How does she have any fight left?
3. She should have given up by now.
4. Who is that boy? Fae don't come here . . .
5. Who is this girl?
6. This is not how Sorrow made it.
7. Hold her down tighter.
8. Wait, she is changing.
9. Is that a tail?
10. Is she a whale? Are those snakes?
11. What magic is this?

(Whimsy the Mermaid)

I flourish a tail as colorful as stained glass
    & whip the bullies' fingers off my scales.

Mama Wata looks on proudly
    folding her arms covered in
endless gold bracelets,
    her snakes bowing at me.

She pushes a broken green
                        sea anemone into my palm.
    Time to hunt, she hisses. *Don't be nice.*
You don't show empathy to those who willfully hurt you.

I swim under the globes & pop up
beside Faerry with legs (again).

His body is bloody
strawberry syrup,
the Garden keeps cutting him.

Faerry's legs buckle,
    his lip lifts.
Are you magic itself, Whimsy?

Hush, I am busy
saving you,
I say.

Faerry collapses against the glass.
Please, by all means, proceed.

I glare at the crowd
Sorrow sent.
My insides boiling hot chocolate.
Time to hunt, I hisssssss . . .

I unmake.
I open my mouth
& cough out a flood
bigger than creation,
a flood of my tears
that for years & years
I never let hit the earth.
The stoners are swept away.

Faerry says,
Now that's a flood.

The water makes me wobble.
I am heavy from magic,
I think I might slip
into the flood.

Faerry grabs me,
wings encompassing

keeping him safe
as the water recedes.
You be the flood—
    I'll be your boat.

CHAPTER 12

DON'T EAT THE APPLE

11:06 PM

Apple Tree:
Boasts wisdom in a fruit,
but sheds it all each year.

(Apples of the Sky)

Faerry holds me & for a moment
the Garden is nowhere,
we are floating in a circle
made from hope & crystal wings.

A distant whistling
  crescendos louder
& a giant apple hits
a patch of foxgloves,
  rocking everything
tossing me from Faerry's cocoon.

We are in the Garden again,
  in the back pocket of Sorrow (again).

An apple orchard surrounds us.

Another apple punches the dirt,
making an apple tree teeter
like a toothpick
in an unbaked pie.

It's going to fall,
I yell as the tree sways
toward us (unsteady).

Faerry magicks & blows wind from his lips.
The tree tumbles the opposite way.

Another apple comes for us
& I tug a breathless Faerry backward.
He tumbles on me, a giant apple lands inches from his leg.

The canopy of trees throws more apples,
the Garden is pounding us with sweetness.

We dodge them & the apples
grow smaller, which is worse.
It is now raining pebble-sized
apples we can't hide from.

I grab one & fling it back at the trees.
The apple rain pauses for a moment.
A woman with black hair & skin whiter than snow
crosses our yellow-bricked path.

You won't last much longer.
The apples won't stop falling.
They never stop falling.
She picks up one of the apples,
takes a bite & wipes her mouth
with her sleeve. *Delicious*, she says,
before falling limp to the ground.

Faerry runs to her.
The apples are poisonous.

Around us the already fallen apples
sizzle on the grass, killing the flowers near them.

Snow White is being bruised by apples—
    when she used to be the apple of everyone's eye.

(Bruises)

Faerry tries to protect the girl,
with skin as white as snow,
from the blows.

A larger apple hits Faerry,
he falls to the ground
his face punched with red
delicious sweetness.
I throw my body over him
& brace for pain,
& it comes, swift & beating.

A black apple bruises my arm
then tumbles to the ground
before rolling toward my fingers.

I think I am supposed
to eat the apple,
I take a sinful bite.

I swallow & the storm shifts.
First to apple cores
then to apple juice rain.
I take another bite, *delicious*.
I eat all the wisdom & place the small core
in the red flannel bag Baba Yaga gave me.

(Riddle)

I stand with my flannel bag filled with an apple core
& three giant black apples sprout from the soil
like onyx pumpkins.
Snow White & Faerry wake.

Snow White points at the three
giant black apples sitting in front
of us.

Each with a door.
Our yellow brick road,
still at our toes,
guiding toward
none of them.

You have to pick one.
Pick well, Snow White says.
    Please pick well.

(Names of Giant Apples)

1. Big Bad Wolf storming again.
2. Adze drinking the blood moon.
3. Rumpelstiltskin, keeper of the nameless.

None of this sounds great.
Faerry turns to Snow White.
You can't give us a hint?

If I could, I would,
but Sorrow has made it this way,
Snow White says.

We go straight. I swallow.
Not left or right, stay the course.
The one in the middle.

Faerry nods.
I trust you.

We lace fingers, thumbs touching
ready to pass through the door.

Snow looks at us like we might have made
a difficult choice, her eyes are wide & worried.

In the silence an apple hits the ground.
Hurry, please hurry! The apple rain comes

hard & Snow White runs into her Garden
looking for a place to hide.

Hand in hand,
Faerry & I
go through the middle
apple's door.

CHAPTER 13

ADZE & THE BLOOD MOON

11:07 PM

Corpse Flower:
Smells like death,
blooms once every 7 years
but is somehow
always alive, alive, alive.

(*Amorphophallus Titanum*: Corpse Flower)

The door is creaky
& the hinges are rusty.

The Garden we enter
into is all shadowy hedges,
except for a giant red owl eye
of a moon spotlighting us in bloody light.
    There are tiny fireflies hovering close
& an occasional hoot
ricocheting through the darkness.

I cover my nose.
What is that scent?

Faerry points to a giant flower
that looks like a dead arm
sticking out of a crimson sea.
    Corpse flower. He coughs.

Hundreds of corpse flowers
litter the Garden,
swaying, looking alive.

Who would want a Garden
of corpse flowers?

A corpse?

Faerry gags.

What do we do now?

Wait? Walk?

We stand in the Garden of stench
surrounded by thousands of fireflies.
Waiting
waiting
waiting
for another
apple to drop
on us.

Waiting for another Fairy Tale—
we wait in fear.

(Never Trust a Firefly)

The fireflies flicker on & off
like blinking eyes.

One lands on Faerry,
he swats it away.
Another lands & bites him,
he crushes it between his fingers.
& a cold shadow rushes at us
(cloudy with a mouth filled with fangs)
before vanishing in thin air.

This is not good.
Faerry swallows
as fireflies land
all over his arms.

My mind races to remember
the name of the creatures
Grandma told me about.
Adze, vampires
that take the shape
of fireflies.

I thought everyone in the Garden
was going to be helpful,
Faerry says, trying not to move.

What do we do?
My eyes widen.

He stays very still, taking the
tiny bites. *Run, Whimsy,*
they have not noticed you yet.

I am not leaving you.
I look at the ground,
our yellow brick road
appears slimmer,
made for one.
Begging me to leave
Faerry to a death
of a thousand bites.

I think this is the only way.

I am not leaving you.
Faerry grows pale,
from the fireflies
drinking his life.

He hits the ground.

An inhale later,
I feel a bite.
Then another.

The fireflies are leaving Faerry.
I run

(I am always running).

    They follow

(I am always being chased).

(Hospital Room)

The bites poke & scratch. Life feels like it lifts in tiny droplets from my body. The fireflies don't stop, my limbs hang heavy, like I might decay, lifeless, into the ground like a leaf. I rip at my hair, wondering if Faerry is still breathing, if I lured the fireflies with fangs for teeth away fast enough.

I sink to my knees & close my eyes tightly, ready to sleep, perhaps forever, until a bright light seeps in. I open my eyes & a hazy vision greets me. I am in a familiar place. Steel laces the windows. I look down, my clothes are clean & white.

I am back in the hospital.

I am stuck in the hospital again.

Crouching on the floor, I am a boat on water, rocking back & forth trying to calm the waves
lapping in me. I count (like they taught me at this hospital)—
one, two, three, four, five . . .
I inhale & exhale (at least ten times).
But I still feel the cold floor under me. I am stuck here again.

I open my eyes & I look up, my hands cover my mouth, pushing a scream back in. Two bodies on steel slabs in the middle of my old hospital room. The room is suddenly so cold that my breath comes out in clouds & smoke. I walk closer, inspecting the lifeless frames, one looks exactly like me (curls & all). The other looks exactly like Faerry (except with cobweb silver wings).

My twin of a corpse opens its eyes & I swear
they are also like mine—
I see myself (looking back at me)—
I see my saddest self
watching me & I remember
what the pit of Depression feels like.

Clinical (Major) Depression

I swallow & start,
I tell my saddest self a story.
I start, even if remembering
shatters me, crumbles me . . .

You felt like funeral drums
banging & banging.

Like a sin, I couldn't talk about you.
So, I was alone,
so alone.

You felt like an undertow
shackled to my ankles,
begging me down,
down,
down.

You turned me into shadow
& stone. Stone in water
sinking,
always sinking.

You were not as quick as quicksand,
you preferred to bite once, twice
let me heal,

then again,
again biting.

You were a scab I could not
stop picking at until I bled.
You made me feel sucked dry.
So dead, I wanted to die.

I look at the Adze
(Grandma taught me
about them)
that looks like me
hunched & zombielike.
But we don't have to do this.
We can keep getting help.

The vampire that looks like me
presents me with the tip
of a stinking flower & I take it
from its cold fingers.

I am Adze, a vampire.
I am magic, but I am never
like the living,
the Adze that looks like me says.

You are not bad.
You are just sad.
We are not bad,
I say.

You know, I was once
a Fairy Tale that everyone knew,
like Snow White & Mama Wata
& all the others.
But joy was
embarrassed by me.
Would not help me.

Sometimes sorrow & joy
exist together.
I place the stinking
flower in the bag.

Not so fast,
you still need the flower stem.
The Adze glares
at the hospital door.
Your friend is coming.

Faerry runs through the door.
& halts, seeing two of me.
One drained & pale,
the other alive,
filled with blood.

He sees the table
& gasps at the other corpse
covered in tiny cuts

with wings like cobwebs
that live in an old window frame—

He sees himself hurting.

(Forgiveness)

The other Adze sits up
& blinks back at us.
Hello, Faerry.

What is going on?
Faerry wets his lips.
I grab his clenched fist.
The Adze reflects back
the parts of you
you are most frightened of.
I think we need to leave.
Faerry pulls me toward the door,
tries to open it, but it's stuck.

You can't get out.
You have to go through me.
The Adze picks at a fresh scab.
Faerry lets go of my hand
rushing toward the vampire
covered in scars (fresh & new).
You can go to hell,
he yells.

This is hell. You can trap
us all here forever,
or you can simply
remind me,
tell me about your pain.
The Adze licks its fangs.

Faerry's jaw is hard.
Then we can go through.
You don't have to face
anything you are not
ready for, Faerry.
Not for me, not for anyone.
The only way out is through.
He sighs as he sits
curls his knees under his chin.
& I want to get through this.
& Faerry begins . . .

(Faerry's Story)

Faerry rocks back & forth,
Sometimes you don't cry
the sorrow out.

Sometimes it takes root
in your bones & in your veins
& spreads to your fingertips.

Sometimes you think you deserve
to feel the pain. Sometimes you think
the pain helps the sadness.

It hurts so much. No one understands—
you are sinking while you are smiling
(at the root of it I was sobbing in every room of my soul).

& no one understands (sometimes)
when your body forgets how to cry
you bleed instead.

Faerry's wings appear & wrap
around him as he rocks back & forth.

Both Adze link hands
& crumble to dust.

They leave a sliver of bone (like a stem)
that I add to my flannel bag.

(Forgiveness Again)

Faerry takes my cheeks
between his hands.
Are you ok?

Yes.
Are you?

He hits his heart.
It hurts. It hurts so much,
remembering.

I nod.
Like lava going into
old wounds.

& we sink (exhausted)
to the ground,
safe with Faerry's wings
like a blanket cocooning us.

CHAPTER 14

VOICELESSNESS & THE SIREN URSULA

11:08 PM

Snapdragons:
Represent deception
& graciousness.
If one can be
deceptively graceful.

(We Stay Cocooned)

We (Faerry & Me) hover here in the hospital room,
airy & waiting for what comes next.

Airy & wondering if maybe with how far we've come,
    here, here, here
       is where we should stay.

Wondering if there are some truths we have forgotten
 & perhaps some we are not ready to face.

It *feels* like we cocoon here until my hair grows,
until my curls reach my toes
& Faerry & I are one like caramel & peanut brittle—inseparable.

Then I open my mouth
to speak & only air comes out—
   Faerry opens his mouth to speak
       & nothing happens.

Our voices have disappeared,
our stories are gone—

I feel it rising
in my throat
Panic.
I am voiceless.

(Ursula: Voice-Taker)

Purple snapdragons grow up the ceiling walls
    & cover the hospital room windows
blocking the view.

I keep trying to talk
but no sounds come out,
voiceless
drowning
in a sea
of purple snapdragons.

Then a woman with a purple shimmering dress
steps through the hospital door—
Hello, Whimsy. Hi, Faerry.
    Cat got your tongue?

I try to answer,
to ask: Where is my voice?
No words climb out
& without my voice—
    I *feel* weaponless.
What is a Conjurer without their voice?

(Thanatosis)

An ocean of flowers
spills through the hospital windows
of the shack of a house.

A siren has stolen my voice.

    I feel it, familiar—
panic,
    panic,
        panic attacks me.

I can't breathe or think.
Panic eats the back of my throat.

Flowers are going to suffocate us.

Faerry's voice startles my mind
        (by some magic)
trying to talk me through,
begging me out of panic
with the marshmallow
undertones of his voice.

It's ok, I understand, breathe,
Faerry says in my mind.

        Then Ursula speaks
        with a drawn-out voice.

You just have to learn
how to come back
to yourself
even when you can't explain
your pain
in this part
of the Garden.

For you, your voice,
your story is everything.

For Faerry,
his voice, comforting you
is everything.

I screw my eyes closed
& feel snapdragons licking
my neck. When my eyes open again,
I can't see anything, just purple
flowers trapping me—
        panic (is itching my bones)
                panic (I can't calm down)
                        panic attacks me.
                                The panic eats me alive.

(Panic Attacks Feel Like . . .)

Between each gasping breath &
before jumping
[*be still* Faerry says softly with his eyes]
the moon blows a bubble,
popping the horizon
breaking a seal
& candy falls out
& the world drowns away.
& gone
going
gone.

I am not sure
anymore what lungs are
[*hush, be still, breathe*
Faerry says with a hug]

I grab Faerry's hand,
tighter. Like I might
fracture his fingers.

& Faerry's wings sprout
holding me like a moonset
that moves like a shawl
over me
& breezes down
nudging the pain (my panic)
out the now open door
into the Garden

[*be still, you have to breathe*
in & out; think about leaves
Faerry insists,
not with words but by guiding
my ear to his chest to listen
to his steady heartbeat]

I try to talk,
panic builds again,
I am stuck
& lies
fall
through the cracks [*I am here*
Faerry says softly
by not letting go]
like sand through
decaying rib cages.

I try to talk & (this time)
a whisper comes out:
Panic has a target
on my back.

The panic feels like
blood & flesh skinned by stone
& water & dirt & all the clocks
screeching an un-clockable time.

[be still (I love you)
please be calm Faerry says by crying]

The Garden is
dead weight.

The Garden is shoving
me down
twisting me into shapes.
Purple snapdragons are everywhere.

[*I see a clearing,*
Faerry says (a real whisper pushed out), *I will carry you*]
I see an opening too, the hospital room is fading.
[*I've got you,* he says
running, moving, running.]

He carries me back
into the Garden with purple snapdragons
instead of corpse flowers.

I can see a bit again,
a snapdragon dances near me,
I grab one to collect & put it in the flannel bag,
I swear it bites—
reminding me, I am here—
still alive,
reminding me that words are not the only language.

CHAPTER 15

THE GRIOT WITH STORIES

11:09 PM

Blackwater Iris:
As black as midnight,
strange & somehow possible
for a short time.

(A Griot)

I un-paralyze from panic
in the clearing
with my head in the crook
of Faerry's arm.

I sit up,
feeling lighter.

The clearing
is hugged by flowers
of every kind.

They start to swirl,
kaleidoscopes into walls
    (not giving us a moment to rest).

A woman with gold fastened
in her hair sits on a giant tree stump
with her legs tucked tightly under her.

I whisper to Faerry,
She's a Griot.
A storyteller.

Her voice is like a thunderbolt.
    You are so close, Whimsy.

I am so tired,
I say, leaning
against Faerry,
Faerry leaning
against me,
us holding
each other up.

All you have
to do now is listen
& watch a very
important story
from three perspectives
with an open heart.
The Griot smiles hopefully.
This Sorrow's Garden is getting weaker.
You are doing well.

We just have to listen?
Faerry exhales
a shaky breath.

You must listen with four ears
& two hearts & at the end
sing into the air the final
truth,
truth,

truth
of it all.

The truth is never
that simple.
I twist my hands.
It can be changed.
Mom used magic
to change our truth
many years ago.

Did she? Or did she not?
No, never simple.
The Griot nods.
So, listen closely.

The leaves fall
from the surrounding trees
like papier-mâché
in a storm & we fall into
the first story.

(Story One: What the Children Saw)

On a thick sheet
of spiderwebs woven
between two giant trees
a movie plays.

Beside the display is Anansi
one leg missing
    (somehow no longer in her Garden)
Anansi begins to narrate:

A girl with licorice hair & a boy with silver wings are playing carelessly in a Forest one day. Their hands are filthy with earth, but their eyes glow. They find a shrub with strawberries & crouch behind it to eat the sweet fruit. It is delicious. Then they hear a voice in the branches of a very tall tree saying, I can't do this anymore. I feel like my soul is sinking out of me. *& another voice saying,* I know, it is like sadness is stuck to me. *The boy with silver wings stops eating his strawberries & the girl with licorice hair squints & sees two people she knows. One of the people in the tree says,* I think of jumping. Maybe I should jump . . .

The boy & girl run, panicked out of their hiding place & are seen by the people in the tree. The boy & girl are worried so they run, they run all the way to their homes to get their parents. Four adults enter the Forest that day. Four adults who tell the girl with licorice hair & the boy with silver wings to stay & wait at the edge. They wait & wait & dig in the dirt until eventually only four adults walk out.

They say, Children, no one is there . . . They must be missing, we will call the police.

They call & search & search for a year, until there is a memorial
& the boy with silver wings & the girl with licorice hair
run into the Forest & cry sad magic
into the soil.

(Falling Again)

Anansi's story ends.
Thousands of large
ants scramble in
to build a stage.

Faerry & I sit
(legs crossed)
in front of the stage
on the soft grass.

I face the stage.
Pay attention,
our lives
all of their lives
depend on it.

Faerry eats a handful
of popcorn.
He has magicked it
for himself.
I am always
paying attention.

(Story Two: What the Parents Saw)

This time Snow White
(also free from her Garden)
steps in from stage right
with bruises from apples still
kissing her skin.

Dear Whimsy, Dear Faerry
I have another story for you.

Four parents are told to leave their homes & come into a forest. They leave their younger children at the edge, afraid of what they might find. They knew their older children were sorrow-filled, they thought it was just a phase when they asked for help. They put them in therapy, but maybe they should have done more.

Four parents stand motionless at the base of a tree in front of two broken bodies. They fall to their knees break
& break & break & decide they can't tell their younger children or they will end up this way too.

So, they call the police & have them taken away. They come out of the forest to say,
Your siblings must be missing . . .
We did not see anything.

They even hire fake investigators. A year later they have a memorial service, but the children know in their bones something is wrong. It's hard to

keep the truth away. So, the mother uses her magic & changes everyone's (the girl, the boy, two fathers, one mother) & her own memories. To the make-believe, they are missing. The boy's family moves.
The girl's family stays, but something feels wrong to the children, they feel like breaking every day.

(Story Three: What Actually Happened)

Baba Yaga hobbles
to the stage.
She snaps her fingers
& the lights
go off & darkness
blinks open
to a scene in a bar.

Her ancient voice tells
a tale of when she was young
& the world wanted so much from her:

A boy & a girl with two younger siblings climbed a tree to get closer to the air. They had been soaked in sadness for some time. They were best friends, talked about everything. How it was hard being different, how they were the only Black ones in school. Sometimes they thought about jumping, one day they said it into the air & their siblings (hiding in the bushes) heard. They rushed down to chase them & tell them it was ok, but a giant branch broke & they fell broken on the ground.

They did not jump.
It was no one's fault,
not even the tree branch.

(Whimsy & Faerry Scream)

It rushes back.
Faerry & I
grasping hands
choking each other's fingers.

The answer,
the root of the root
& the vine of the vine
is not a word.

It's not
a phrase.

It's a wail,
a screech.
A howl
that cuts through ears
slices through the sky
like a shooting star.

There is no one to blame,
not the branch, the siblings,
not the parents . . .

Faery & I scream & wail into the silence.
It stabs the Garden
in its center,
draining it of water,

of magic,
of life.

It's a wail.
A howl.
A shout
& a look
through bloodshot eyes
& matted hair.

A look with a set jaw
that says
Not today, Sorrow.
Not tomorrow.
Not ever again.

& Baba Yaga grins
drumming her metal nose.

A Blackwater Iris
appears & I grab it.

The last circle will test you . . . ,
Baba Yaga says.
Remember you don't have to be brave,
you lived,
you are (both)
already bravery itself.

CHAPTER 16

FAERRY (TALE) & WHIMSY (COLE)

11:10 PM

Skeleton Flower:
Has white innocent petals
until tears hit them
& the petals become
translucent.
The petals disappear—
Sometimes things disappear.

(Bigger Than Bravery)

Baba Yaga swishes her hand in the air
& the Garden swirls & spins into a rainbow
of colors & flowers mixing.

Then it all stops
& we are on hot pavement
surrounded by black hyacinth,
as steam sizzles off the road.

The ground thunders & a giant beech tree sprouts.
    Faerry & I both misplace our voices—
we both hover weightless watching
a white & a gray owl
cling to the highest branches.

Then jump
    don't flap their wings once—
& crumble on the ground.

We flinch,
    like an earthquake
has rippled our bones.

We should help them,
I say, walking toward
the broken owls.

I hope they are ok,
Faerry says,
shrugging off his jacket.

We reach the owls,
white & gray like a balance.

I kneel, pulling the gray one
    into my arms, its large yellow eyes familiar.

Faerry wraps the white one in his jacket.
    The owls don't move, but their eyes track us.

A great gust of wind sweeps over the Garden
like an ocean's wave & branches fall
like tears from the tree.

We cradle the owls,
scrambling from the tree
as it crumbles & decays like a virus
has taken root in it.

The owls grow warm in our arms,
    like fire, so warm we have to let go,
so warm they catch fire, burn blue
& golden amber.

From the ashes
two hazy haunts step out—
    Tale & Cole.

(Tale & Cole)

Their ghosts haven't aged a day
    their clothes are just as I remember—
Cole wears gray leather gloves & Tale's hair
is held back by a pair of pink sunglasses.

Tale?
Faerry's voice
is a long shadow.

Cole?
My voice is a dull wind.

They stand together, fingers twined.
    Smiling. Haunting.

I run to Cole's ghostly form,
expecting it to turn to a cloud
but when my arms wrap around him
it's warm, my head tucks under his chin—
    Cole says, *I've missed you so much,*
        Whimsy.

Faerry steps cautiously toward his sister,
reaches out his fingers. Tale reaches too, pulls Faerry into a hug.
    He is taller than her now.
(We have changed, they have not.)
Tale's head rests under Faerry's chin.
She says, *Baby bro . . . I've missed you.*

(We've Been Watching You)

Cole holds me at arm's length.
You've grown taller.

Are you real?
I ask.

Ancestors are always real, Whimsy—
Grandma taught us that.
Cole squeezes my hand.

Are you leaving again?
I say
hands shaking.

The ones you love, don't leave—
they just come back different.
Cole squeezes a gray owl feather
into the palm of my hand.
Add this to your flannel bag.

Tale hands Faerry a white owl feather—
You've grown very tall, Faerry.

Faerry holds the feather like it is gold.
You've been watching over us?
he asks. She nods.

I am so sorry.
You should still be here.
I cry.

It's no one's fault.
Not yours.
Not the tree,
Cole says.

Not the ground
that broke us,
Tale adds.

We didn't jump.
We fell,
they say (together).

(Truth)

It's not our fault?
I whisper.

It's not our fault,
Faerry repeats.

Tale & Cole answer:
You saved us.
You found us.

We've been here,
as ghosts, tied to the Garden
feeling guilty for so long.

& I run into my brother's ghost's arms (again).
& Faerry runs into his sister's ghost's arms (again).

Faerry & Tale (Fairy Tale).
Whimsy & Cole (Whimsical).

THE REBIRTH

The ancient Bennu bird of Egypt, often associated with the soul of Ra, resembled a heron with a white crown. It sat atop the Benben Stone—the Mound of Creation the only solid ground in a universe not yet created.

It sat soundless in darkness—
alone, waiting & (perhaps) wilting—
then the Bennu bird's cry broke
through the silence & darkness
& its cry decided creation
& light began to trickle in
slowly.

But that is not the end of the story.
Each day the Bennu bird renews with the sun—
wiser—ready to fly
ready to soar
ready to live
wildly & vastly
like Whimsy & Faerry.

CHAPTER 17

FAIRY TALES IN THE SECRET GARDEN

11:11 PM

High John the Conquer Root: Overcomes all obstacles.

(Candy House: Final Time)

A door appears & we all
(Faerry, Tale, Cole & Me)
walk through & are at the start again.

Sorrow's beard is gray.
With red eyes
it opens its mouth
coughs up salt—
You ruined it all.

The Garden grows smaller
the door (to the candy house)
opens & closes
several times as Fairy Tale
women surround
Sorrow.

Baba Yaga stands, hands on hips.
We have work to do.

Baba Yaga ties
the flannel bag with the flowers
I collected around
the neck of Sorrow.

We surround Sorrow that is
gray & coughing.

Some of us have deep cuts,
some of us have black eyes.
But we are all here
here
here. All of us (alive).

All of us,
Baba Yaga
Anansi
Mama Wata
Snow White
Adze the vampire
Ursula the Siren
the Griot,
Faerry's sister, Tale (as a haunt)
My brother, Cole (ghostly & strong)
Faerry (with silver wings) & Me (Whimsy).

Baba Yaga pours the fuel
laced with High John the Conquer Root,
& uses it as kindling for the flames.

We use the lost leg
of Anansi as a match & set
the candy house on fire.

We lock Sorrow
in the candy house it built
          to burn.

I pull my notebook from my backpack
use an eraser & smudge out Sorrow's name.

Chocolate melts ruddy
& rotting.

Through the candy window
I see the skin of Sorrow
alter red & red & redder—
like a fireball candy about to explode.

We watch.
    We watch together.
Tale & Cole (shadowy)
standing behind us all
watching the Garden,
making sure nothing half alive slithers out—
    hope growing thick
          in all of us.

(Explosion)

The candy house
explodes glitter,
dust settles.

We jump
holler & shout
          in the clearing—
                    we conquered Sorrow (again).

(Fairy Tales Celebrate in the Garden Sorrow Built)

We are shaking & free
& imperfect but hopeful.

We, the Fairy Tales,
the patron saints
    of lost causes.

We have been stoned & burned,
but slow & steady wins the race.

It is like the bullet Sorrow meant for us
            stopped midair
    smoky & utterly confused.

We won. We found the way
    (all of us).

We will cry telling this story
of seven women (magical)
one giant spider
& a boy (Fae),
& Tale & Cole
(ghosts set free)
strutting out
of a Forest,
full moon like
a lemon cookie in the sky.

We've stepped out, shades hiding our tired eyes,
leather gloves covering our magical hands.
We broke the Garden that Sorrow built.

Prowlers on a walkabout—
ready to roam,
ready to live, thrive, live . . .

(To Home We Go)

My parents are still
    at a Halloween party
(time was strange in the Garden).
11 minutes felt like 11 hours.
Sometimes sorrow is like that.

Cole & Tale (haunting)
sit at the kitchen table
looking hazy
& explain—
    We cried when you heard us.
We got stuck in the Garden (together).
We could not get out. Even as ghosts.
    We've missed you so much.

I didn't understand then.
Sorrow is no one's fault,
I say.

Faerry hugs his sister.
Will you disappear?

Yes, Tale says.

But we will haunt
    you whenever you like,
        Cole adds.

EPILOGUE:

HAPPY ENDINGS

WHIMSY & FAERRY

Daffodil:
New beginnings.
New chances.
New joy.

(Whimsy & Faerry)

Faerry stays with me—
we sink exhausted on my bedroom floor,
Faerry's wings cocoon me & we sleep.

I wake up beside Faerry,
glowing & renewed.

He is warm. He is good. He is safe.
He opens an eye.

I say,
Hello, bonjour . . .

Faerry faces me.
Hello, Hello, Hello, Whimsy.

I trace his lifeline
with my thumb.
Let's write our story,
so no one can take it away.

Faerry's hand with black-painted nails
strokes my cheek.
Whimsy & Faerry beat the Garden.

Burned it to the ground,
I whisper.

Saved our siblings' ghosts
(Tale & Cole),
Faerry adds.

& some pretty impressive
Fairy Tales,
I brag.

& ourselves.
(again).
Faerry leans in closer to me.

We did have help.
Our foreheads touch.
Help is always good.

Faerry nods, agreeing.
& my palms glow
brighter than the moon,
his wings like silver glittering stars.

Faerry ruffles my hair.
Hello, hello, hello,
best (Hoodoo) friend.

I tap his nose
three times saying,
Hi. Hi. Hi,
best (Fae) friend.

Narrator (Interlude)

Do you understand now (reader)?
There is someone out there rooting for you.
You are not alone, in any Forest.
You there, *hello, bonjour, hola*—
we are rooting,
cheering for you
to live & thrive.

AUTHOR'S NOTE

Clinical depression affects over 16 million American adults yearly. The statistics worldwide are staggering: an estimated 264 million suffer from depression worldwide—myself included.

Many examples in Sorrow's Garden are taken from my own personal experiences dealing with death at a very young age & the trauma that rippled from those experiences. When I was in third grade, one of my friends passed away after falling off a swing. Several other difficult & painful occurrences followed. Experiences I never fully faced. Instead I buried the pain down in the roots of me. Everyone carries trauma differently. It was not until eleventh grade, after the death of another friend, that the pain came rippling down. It took me until I was twenty-four to get the help & therapy I needed. I wish I had asked for help sooner. Before I reached out for help, the only place I found comfort was in words, stories & Fairy Tales.

Stories keep the world intact. Storytelling predates the written word by more than 3,000 years. Fairy Tales, specifically, have always protested against societal constraints & commented on the human condition. Fairy Tales offer whimsy & truth—the whimsy makes us brave & the truth points us in the right direction. I used Fairy Tales from around the world in this novel because they remind me of hope & they also show that no one, not even Baba Yaga or Anansi the spider, is immune to sorrow. Fairy Tales help us process great pain & make sense of our own inner struggles. The circles of the Garden represent the layers of depression—the endless memories, traumas & pain that play in our minds constantly.

I want everyone to know that there are people who want to help. If you need someone to talk to, there are hotlines open 24/7. There are nonprofit organizations that are committed to helping. You are not alone.

National Suicide Prevention Lifeline
https://suicidepreventionlifeline.org
1-800-273-8255

Substance Abuse and Mental Health Services Administration
www.samhsa.gov/find-help/national-helpline
1-800-662-HELP (4357)

To Write Love on Her Arms (nonprofit)
https://twloha.com

GLOSSARY OF FAIRY TALES, STORIES & FOLKLORE

Adze: A creature from Ewe folklore. It presents in the form of a firefly & will turn into a human being when captured. Adzes are essentially shape-shifting vampires. They can also possess people & turn them into witches.

Anansi: The West African trickster god who takes the form of a spider. There were no stories until Anansi brought them from the sky god. Anansi possesses vast knowledge & knows all stories.

Baba Yaga: One of the most well-known beings in Slavic folklore, she is a supernatural woman with boundless power. She is often described as having a metal nose, living in a hut with chicken legs. She may help or hurt those she encounters & is both feared and respected.

Bennu bird: A bird that looks like a heron & in Egyptian culture is said to have started creation from its cry. It is also believed to be the inspiration for the myth of the phoenix rising from its ashes.

Bluebeard: A character in a French folktale, a man with a blue beard, who tells his wife not to open one locked chamber in his mansion. Eventually his wife unlocks the chamber & finds the bodies of all the previous wives Bluebeard has murdered.

Fae: Highlighted throughout European folklore & mythology, Fae describes a group of ethereal, magical & sometimes mischievous individuals. Many beings fall under the umbrella of Fae, including banshees, elves, goblins, leprechauns, tiny fairies & many more. Some have wings & some do not. The uniting characteristic of Fae are their magical abilities.

Godmother Death: A character inspired by a story by the Brothers Grimm in which a man with thirteen children decides to make death their godfather instead of god or the devil, because death takes both the rich & the poor.

Griot: Perhaps the most important keeper of the oral tradition of storytelling, a griot is a West African storyteller responsible for preserving a community's history, recording births, telling stories & often advising royalty.

"Hansel & Gretel": A German Fairy Tale about two siblings, Hansel & Gretel, who are abandoned in a dark forest. Trying to find their way home, they come across a gingerbread house belonging to a witch who likes to eat children. They trick the witch & eventually escape.

Hoodoo/Conjure/Rootwork: An African American magic system that arose in the Americas after enslaved Africans were stolen from their homelands & stripped of their way of life. Hoodoo & its many practices are as unique as the regions they took root in, but the pillars of Hoodoo include: the elevation of ancestors; knowledge of & working with herbs, roots, candles, sticks & bones; oneness with nature; & balance.

Inferno: A fourteenth-century epic poem written by Dante that outlines his journey through Hell guided by the poet Virgil. In the poem, Hell has many circles—each reserved for a different sin.

Mama Wata: A West African water spirit associated with fertility & life. She is known for kidnapping her followers & bringing them to her realm for a long time. When they leave, they acquire wealth & become more beautiful.

Snow White: Known for eating a poisoned apple & falling into a deep slumber until awakened by true love's kiss, she is hated by her stepmother for her beauty. When her stepmother asks a magical mirror, *Who is the fairest in all of the land*, the mirror answers, *Snow White*.

Ursula (Sirens): Ursula is known in the Disney film *The Little Mermaid* for taking Ariel's voice, but her existence is a clear reference to Sirens, who lure men to their deaths with their beautiful singing.

The Yellow Brick Road: In the 1939 film *The Wizard of Oz*, Dorothy must follow a yellow brick road to find her way back home, to Kansas.

FAIRY TALES IN THIS STORY

Cole & Tale: Two best friends whose siblings heard them speaking about their sadness. The friends fell from a large water beech tree, tried to get to their siblings & their ghosts got stuck in a magical Garden crafted from the Fairy Tales found in a notebook.

The Forest with the Garden: A magical Garden crafted from the Fairy Tales found in a notebook. The Garden sprouted from the sorrow of a girl who practiced Hoodoo after she cried a puddle at the base of a water beech tree. The Garden is a metaphor for the layers of clinical depression.

Whimsy & Faerry: Two best friends, a Conjurer & a Fae, heard their siblings talking about death. The friends ran to their parents for help, but when their parents arrived at the beech tree, they claimed no one was there & that their siblings were missing. Whimsy creates, & gets stuck in, a magic Garden crafted from her sorrow. It is filled with characters from her Fairy Tale notebook. Whimsy & Faerry must travel through the Garden to escape Sorrow.

WHIMSY & FAERRY'S PLAYLIST

1. "The Longer I Run" by Peter Bradley Adams
2. "Are You All Good?" by breathe.
3. "A Change Is Gonna Come" by Sam Cooke
4. "La Di Da" by Lennon Stella
5. "Edge of the Dark" by Emmit Fenn
6. "XO" by Beyoncé
7. "I Put a Spell On You" by Nina Simone
8. "Move with Me" by Locals Only Sound
9. "Without Fear" by Dermot Kennedy
10. "Would That I" by Hozier
11. "Strange" by Agust D & RM

ACKNOWLEDGMENTS

The journey to finishing this novel truly took a village & I am infinitely grateful for every single stunning soul that planted the seeds of encouragement that allowed *We Are All So Good at Smiling* to bloom into the book it is now.

As always, countless thanks to the ancestors & more specifically to Lucille Clifton, who wrote a line of poetry that is gospel & continues to guide my soul: "come celebrate / with me that everyday / something has tried to kill me / and has failed." I found this poem when I was 24, when I never thought I'd make it to 25 or 26 & I thought, *I can celebrate today, for being here now*—this moment is enough. I believe poetry is magic & this line awakened something in me & encouraged me to seriously seek the help I needed.

To my parents, to put it simply, I am (still) here because of you. Thank you for loving me so thoroughly, vastly & unconditionally. Thank you for teaching me that love is a medicine that can amplify all others.

Monica, bestie, we've been on this yellow brick road together for a long time. I feel like we've entered, gotten stuck in & escaped many haunted forests (literally & figuratively). Let's keep adventuring forever while listening to BTS, Hozier & Beyoncé.

Cristian Dennis, you are (always) poetry in brilliant motion. Thank you for bringing so much joy into my life.

Ally, wonderful human, your haunted house book made me brave enough to write this—thank you.

To my agent, Rena Rossner, thank you for always seeing the heart in my stories & to my editor, Liz Szabla, a thousand times thank you for guiding me through crafting this book. Many thanks to the entire team at Feiwel & Friends.

To you, reader, thank you for picking up this book about depression & pain & hope. I am always wishing you well.

Thank you for reading this Feiwel & Friends book. The friends who made WE ARE ALL SO GOOD AT SMILING possible are:

Jean Feiwel, Publisher

Liz Szabla, VP, Associate Publisher

Rich Deas, Senior Creative Director

Holly West, Senior Editor

Anna Roberto, Senior Editor

Kat Brzozowski, Senior Editor

Dawn Ryan, Executive Managing Editor

Allene Cassagnol, Production Manager

Emily Settle, Editor

Rachel Diebel, Editor

Foyinsi Adegbonmire, Associate Editor

Brittany Groves, Assistant Editor

Michelle McMillian, Designer

Lelia Mander, Production Editor

Follow us on Facebook or Twitter and visit us online at mackids.com. Our books are friends for life.